"Loved *Burning Justice*! What a great wrap up to the Chasing Fire Alaska series. Romantic suspense lovers will enjoy this story and this series, highly recommend!"

—Jeanne, Goodreads

"I'm not going to lie, I'm sad that this series has come to an end. A fast paced suspense that is perfect for the ending of this series! I devoured this one!"

—Laramee, Goodreads

"What an epic ending to the Chasing Fire: Alaska series. Kane and Maria's story is fast-paced and a wild adventure. Filled with intrigue, danger, and action, *Burning Justice* will not leave you disappointed. I loved the backstories of Kane and the Troubled Boys. Phillips crafted an amazing suspense read containing Christian elements."

—Allyson, Goodreads

BURNING JUSTICE

CHASING FIRE ALASKA | BOOK 6

BURNING JUSTICE

LISA PHILLIPS

sunrise
PUBLISHING

Burning Justice
Chasing Fire: Alaska, Book 6

Print ISBN: 978-1-966463-04-7

For more information about Lisa Phillips please access the author's website at www.authorlisaphillips.com.
Published in the United States of America.
Cover Design: Sunrise Media Group LLC

· CHASING FIRE ALASKA ·

Burning Hearts
Burning Rivals
Burning Escape
Burning Secrets
Burning Truth
Burning Justice

To all of you who stick with us authors to the end, to the last book in a series. We hope it was a satisfying ride! But you have to know... Is it ever really over? See you all soon!

Before the mountains were brought forth,
or ever you had formed the earth and the world,
from everlasting to everlasting you are God.

PSALM 90:2 ESV

ONE

ALMOST A DECADE AS A SPY FOR the CIA hadn't prepared Maria Sanchez one bit for this life. Fighting wildfires in the Alaskan backcountry. Trying to stop a dangerous militia group from deploying a biological weapon on US soil.

Okay, so that last one was a bit more her speed.

Still, talk about being unprepared.

Kind of like the way she felt every time *he* looked at her. Kane Foster. Broody. Quiet. A former soldier, a guy who put loyalty above everything.

Cue heart fluttering.

Until the rumble of thunder split the sky, growing like a wave until it crested right on top of them. It sounded so close that Maria ducked, tucking her knees up to her chest and holding on tight. The way her father had always told her to. She tipped her head back against the mossy tree to watch the sky light up over Denali Mountain.

"There you are."

She flinched and turned to look over her shoulder but didn't uncurl her limbs. The night air had a chill.

"Need my sweater?" Kane reached for his zipper. Dark-blond hair, short on the sides but with the top sticking out all over because he didn't care to fix it. Stubble across his chin because he didn't care about that either. But the man cleaned up good on a Friday night, that was for sure.

She shook her head. The point was to *not* need anything, because needing things from people never ended well.

He settled beside her on the ground, close enough that she could feel his warmth. "Impressive storm."

She turned back to the sky stretched out in front of them. Above them. "This was a good place to stop for the night."

Kane nudged her elbow. "That means you're supposed to be getting some sleep, like everyone else."

"I signed up to take watch. Keep an eye on the fire."

"Right." His low chuckle drifted over. "That's why you're hiding over here, pretending you're alone in the dark."

"It's not as impressive if you feel safe. Storms are supposed to be dangerous and out of control. You're supposed to be a little afraid."

"Don't worry, I am."

Maria didn't think he was talking about the weather—or wildland firefighting. They'd been doing that for two seasons now. Laying low. Pretending they were regular folks who wanted a career change. Anything other than what they actually were.

Or why they were out here.

"Fear is a tool." Lightning cracked across the sky, making her pause before she continued. "It keeps you sharp. If you don't learn how to control it, you'll get swallowed up."

The storm whipped up some wind, blowing through the valley below and ruffling her hair across her face. The ever-present tang of burnt wood hung on the breeze. An odd, discordant presence that reminded her every second that the fire on the horizon was destroying property and vegetation, growing. Moving. Flames that seemed to flicker with life, trying to devour everything in its path.

She slid the dark strands that had come loose from her ponytail behind her ear. How well she knew fire, and the knowledge she had should be an asset and not a liability here.

After everything she'd been through, there had to be good. All the team members who studied the Bible now, talking about God working all things for good.

Whatever Kane thought about what she'd said about fear, he didn't share with her. He sat quietly, hopefully enjoying the night now that the sun had finally set. In three or four hours, it would rise again.

Of course she was going to sit out here trying to figure out how to solve all this.

"I thought about giving up, you know." Talk about fear. She barely even wanted to admit it. "He's been gone nearly fifteen years. I wondered if he wanted to be gone. If he chose to stay away."

"Now you know that was never true."

"But I believed it." She winced. "I would've quit because I lost the faith that I would ever find him. That I would get my father back."

A couple of weeks ago, a reporter had seen her father being held at gunpoint. Maria was closer to finding her father now than she'd been in fifteen years.

"I feel like every time we get somewhere with the search, we immediately get knocked back three steps." She ducked her head, ashamed to say she was losing the strength to fight. "We can't keep chasing him forever and live our lives. By the time we find him, he's gone. Moved on."

Kane nudged her elbow with his. "We didn't get this close only to lose him now."

"You said that in Montana, and he was gone before we found where they were keeping him." Maria turned to look at him and realized his face was closer than she'd thought. In the dark, she could barely make out his features.

But she didn't need the light to know what he looked like. She'd spent nearly two years with this man. His green eyes. His furrowed brow and crossed arms when he needed to think in silence. The two-day stubble across his jaw. His broad shoulders that made her want to curl up in his arms and let him impart some of that strength to her.

"I have to find him," Maria said. "Before it costs me the rest of my life."

Kane cleared his throat. "None of us is going to quit. You're not fighting alone. We all agreed to do this together."

"Right." The team.

The Trouble Boys. Hammer, Saxon, and Kane. Members of the same Delta Force unit. Brothers who had fought and bled—and been declared dead—side by side. And Hammer's little brother, Mack. The kid no one wanted to leave behind.

Her protectors. Her family.

Kane tossed a small stone a few feet away. "You should get some sleep. I'll take watch. It's going to be a long day tomorrow if we're gonna quash this fire before it can jump the highway."

"You're right."

He stood and held out his hand. She reached up and grabbed his wrist where he had the tattoo of his unit under a leather cuff. Let him pull her to her feet. They both let go like a spark of static electricity had hit them. But it never did—because they didn't allow it to go that far. Hammer had made it clear that getting distracted and exposing themselves could cost them all a future. Fighting wildfires was a great way to stay off the grid while they continued their search for Doctor Cortez and the man who'd betrayed them.

First following leads in Montana.

Now up here in Alaska.

Since their team had been declared killed in action on the same day they'd rescued Maria from captivity in Syria, they'd been trying to get their lives back. It hadn't taken long to realize doing so wouldn't be all that easy—namely because they'd been attacked almost immediately after leaving and Kane had been captured.

They'd barely made it out of Syria alive, but they'd learned something important.

Someone powerful didn't want them to see the light of day.

At that point, they hadn't even known about the plan in the works, the threat to the country that they knew now they had to stop. All they'd known was that they had to lay low long enough to figure out what had happened.

Back then it had been about finding the man who'd betrayed them. Who'd held Maria, and then Kane, and cost them all their lives.

After they'd gone looking for answers and discovered her father's name on a stolen report, they'd quickly realized it was also about finding Doctor Cortez. The fact she and Kane had been nursing these feelings for each other had nothing to do with the mission parameters. Giving in was a temptation that didn't help them reach their goals—a distraction that could cost them the future.

Now that they knew it was all connected, the guys were as invested in this plan to set everything back to rights as she was. Joining forces with them meant she had to not jeopardize their chance to restore their reputations and get their lives back.

She walked by him. "Good night, Kane."

"Good night, Sanchez."

Another peal of thunder rumbled across the sky. As much as she wanted to pretend she was alone, just her and nature in all its destructive power, she hadn't been alone for a while now. She might have lost a lot, but what she'd gained were men who would risk everything to help her. Who believed as she did that the world was worth saving and that good people should be able to live in peace and safety.

Maria picked her way between the trees, over to the spot where the rest of the hotshots had chosen to make camp for the night. Basic bedrolls had been laid out, packs for pillows. She spotted the outlines of her boys and the empty spot for Kane. Hammer lifted his head as she passed, so Maria signaled with a handwave that everything was fine.

She passed the spots where Mitch—their hotshot crew chief—and Grizz lay a few feet from each other. Grizz had an e-reader out, the backlight shining on his face. Apparently, whatever he was reading was hilarious.

At the far end, the only other woman, Raine Josephs, snored quietly. Maria lay down on her bedroll and looked at the hazy sky, the stars obscured by smoke from the wildfire that had flared to life the day before.

Somewhere out there, her father was being held captive.

Years in the CIA hadn't given her a lead as to who was responsible. The men who had shot her mother in front of her and then taken her father from her went unpunished because she hadn't ever managed to find their identities. Only evidence that her father had been used for his skills and then sold to someone else. The first transaction in a chain she'd been able to track. Always one step behind actually finding him.

This personal mission had driven her ever since. It had led to her capture in Syria, where she'd come face-to-face with the enemy. At the time, she hadn't known who he was—outside of her personal connection to him. Her *asset.*

Despite the Trouble Boys not wanting her to be his target again, she'd found out what she needed to know about who the man was. And what he had done.

Three weeks after her capture, she'd been rescued by a Delta Force unit who'd been betrayed by people who should've had their backs. All because their teammate had sold them out, they'd landed in a mission that nearly got them all killed.

These men had fought for her.

Stuck with her.

Called her family.

They'd never given up.

Maria swiped tears from her face. Their fight had become hers. Her fight had become theirs.

If she didn't figure out how to finish it soon, she could lose them all.

Day seven hundred thirteen of being dead started like any other day. Kane Foster tied the laces on his boots and didn't bother to run his hands through his hair. It wasn't like there was a mirror out here.

He glanced at Mack. "Ready?"

The kid was twenty as of last week, and finally quit texting long enough to realize Kane was talking to him. "What—yep, ready." He unfolded those wiry limbs and stood, his features darker than his older brother Hammer.

"How is Alexis today?" Who else would the kid be texting other than a certain young woman he'd met last summer?

Mack eyed him. "How is Sanchez?"

Kane shoved his shoulder. "Bet you can't beat me to the trailhead." He swiped up his pack and took off running west, to the spot where the others had gathered. The carb-loaded breakfast sat heavy in his stomach, but he would need all the energy for the day. He hadn't lied to Sanchez about that.

Mack caught up, his dark eyes and long lashes far too knowing. "Alexis is fine, by the way."

"Good. She's at the teens camp?"

"Wildlands Academy, yeah." Mack nodded. "She said they took a field trip and fought a fire from a train with a water tank car. They rode the train and sprayed the fire."

"And now you wanna put out a fire from a train?"

Mack glanced over. "Don't you?"

"Okay, fair point," Kane said. "That would be cool."

"She also found out she got a job as an EMT in Bozeman, so she's moving in a couple of weeks."

"Tell her I said well done, yeah?"

Mack nodded, and Kane spotted the pinch of frustration at the edge of his expression. The kid had met Alexis last year in Montana. She was the daughter of a buddy of theirs, a firefighter from

Last Chance County who'd joined the Ember crew as a hotshot. One of the smokejumpers here in Alaska, Orion Price, was Alexis's half brother. Mack had earned a lot of respect—and it was probably why Charlie let the kid text with his daughter.

Kane said, "Patience is a good thing. Same with not being reckless when the most likely outcome is that someone gets hurt."

Mack walked beside him to the trailhead, over the uneven, rocky ground normally traversed by four-legged creatures. Not so many two-legged, except them. "Still sucks."

"But it's the right thing. She might be eighteen now, but she's still young." Kane reached over and squeezed the back of the kid's neck. "You know where she is when the time is right."

"Pretty sure it'll be right as soon as the season is done. If the mission is finished then."

"I get you." Kane chuckled. "And I hope the mission is finished as well. Being dead is getting old."

They caught up to the rest of the hotshots and started the hike to the fire line.

Kane's phone buzzed in his pocket. It was almost as if thinking about family connections had summoned a text from his cousin in Last Chance County.

Kane would have to wait until less people were around before reading and responding to it, something Ridge knew well enough. His cousin never called. He let Kane call him when he could do it without anyone knowing. Even if it didn't matter that these people knew he and Ridge were related.

What mattered was that the world kept believing Kane, Hammer, and Saxon were dead.

Juggling all the secrets was becoming tiresome. Although, his feelings for Sanchez weren't a secret. Everyone knew how he felt about her, and most of the people they worked with presumed she felt the same about him. But the need to maintain focus and not cross any lines meant he worked hard to compartmentalize it all. She would never be *Maria.* She would always be *Sanchez.*

Once he tumbled off that cliff, it would be a long way down. Kane would never get back up.

Kind of like Mack with the young woman he'd fallen for, the timing had to be right.

Still, Kane had never been a fan of "yes but not yet" from the Lord.

Waiting sucked as much as having to search locations one by one, eliminating each in turn.

Narrowing down the search for her father. The search for a canister of dangerous toxin their enemy—the man who had betrayed his team—wanted to use to destabilize the US.

Mack jogged up to walk beside his brother, Hammer. Saxon chatted with Raine, the two of them walking beside each other.

Grizz and Mitch were in the lead.

Sanchez stepped off to the side and looked at the sky. She'd pulled her dark hair back today, and it shone in the morning sun. High cheekbones. A slender figure but with so much strength packed into it from fighting wildfires that it sometimes seemed like she could withstand anything. When he'd caught up to her, she joined him at the back of the line. Like it was no big deal to stop and wait for him. Almost like she wanted to be near him.

Kind of like the way he wanted to be near her.

"So where are we headed today?" He didn't glance at her. *Play it cool and no one gets burned.*

"Because you weren't listening to the briefing, you were talking to Mack?" She motioned to the kid, up ahead, tossing rocks off the trail every twenty feet or so.

Really? The kid was just walking through the backcountry, chucking rocks like this was a stroll?

Kane focused back on Maria—and caught the

disgruntled look on her face. He chuckled. "Hit me with the highlights."

She kept pace with him, her strength clearer in the lines of her muscles now than it had been when they met. She'd always been strong, but the physical nature of this work had brought a lot more of that strength to the surface.

It was enough to make a guy think he had heart problems.

If the woman ever dressed up to go out, he wasn't sure he'd survive.

"The North Fire is zero-percent contained. It's headed for a thirty-acre patch of trees that got infested with some bug that ate them all from the inside out. There's no moisture and a bunch of dry tinder. If the fire swallows that, it'll grow, and the whole place will go up like a barn full of hay."

"Is that right?"

She shoved his shoulder. "I can speak back-country."

"You were born in San Diego."

"There are farms there!"

Kane busted up laughing. "Sure, sure."

"And I'm supposed to believe you're a regular blue-collar guy from Last Chance County? Because I've met more than one of those the past couple of years, and you're . . . something different."

"Is that right?"

"Commendations. Medals. The only reason you don't have a Purple Heart is because you're supposedly dead."

"Mmm. Shame." He rolled his shoulders, more of a reflex than anything else. "I don't want recognition over what happened. This is far from done."

But in his heart and mind, he had to acknowledge it, because he knew better than anyone that ignoring stuff or burying it just meant more trouble later.

Their team had been betrayed.

"You don't want a medal because you think it was your fault." She glanced aside at him. "Even though it wasn't. You guys were there to rescue me. You had no idea—"

"Neither did you," Kane said.

"So neither of us is at fault."

"We've been over this."

Sanchez sighed. "You rescued me, and you were betrayed."

"Now ask me what we'd have done if we knew going in that it was a trap. So I can tell you we'd have done it anyway. We'd have rescued you even if we knew it would work out like this."

She shook her head but said nothing.

"And when Hammer realized Mack was at home, living under his father's thumb—the worst kind of place to be—we picked him up and brought him with us. Because we don't let people fall through the cracks. Everyone deserves to have someone show up for them. You, me, and Mack."

He continued, "Now we're going to do the same with your father. And we're going to find the people behind the Sons of Revolution militia and finish this. When it's all done, we're going to get our lives back."

"I hope so." She said it so quietly he almost didn't hear it.

The line of hotshots slowed, and Mitch stepped off the trail, toward the tree line.

"I guess we're here." Kane knew for a fact there was a snowcapped mountain in front of them, but the thick wildfire smoke made it invisible. Enclosed them in a cloud that hung like fog on the horizon and caused a scratch in his throat that he had to cough out.

Saxon walked back to them. "Everything okay?"

Kane and Saxon had been in boot camp together. They'd fought, sweated, and bled together. Now they were dead together. It brought a certain clarity to everything he did. Who had time to beat around the bush when the fate of a country was on the line?

"Everything is fine. What's with the location?" Kane motioned up the trail and spotted Mack right as he tossed another rock.

He knew Saxon didn't buy that he was fine, but he didn't challenge Kane. "Mitch said there's a cabin through the—"

An explosion rocked the ground under them. Fire, smoke, and dirt sprayed into the air, caught a tree and sent it skyward in pieces.

All of them ducked into a crouch.

The last one down was Raine, looking around at him and Saxon. "What was that?"

"No one move!" Everything in Kane went cold. "That was a land mine."

TWO

MARIA SPUN AROUND IN HER crouch, wobbled, and landed on her butt in the dirt. “What? He said *land mine*.”

Saxon turned that dark stare on her. When he wanted to be, he could be scary, but the guy was a teddy bear. Earlier in the season, they’d come across an evacuating family with a deaf child, and he’d spent an hour hiking alongside the kid, conversing in sign language until the kid had snorted because he was laughing so hard at Saxon’s jokes.

Over by the trees, Mitch called out, “Everyone good?”

They each sounded off. Raine’s voice wavered, and both Hammer and Mack turned to face her—but Maria couldn’t hear what they were saying.

Mitch yelled, "No one moves until we figure this out."

Maria looked from him to Saxon, then Kane, who had crouched closer to her. "I feel like I should check under my feet and around me. Just to make sure."

"Quicker to toss rocks and set them all off." Saxon turned to face up the trail, eyeing the ground between him and Raine. He yelled, "I told you we should get a K-9!"

Grizz looked as unhappy as he normally did, but the typical grumpy expression on his face had softened a lot since he'd met Dani. Right now? The mountain man surveyed the area around them between the trail and the two fields of tall spruce.

Maria checked the dirt around her. "I don't think there are any land mines on the trail. We would've hit one before now."

She was ready to thank God that they hadn't but wasn't sure if she wanted to open that can of worms. Kane believed in God and said he trusted Him. Even after everything he'd been through, he held tight to his faith. It impressed her enough she'd considered it, purely because by all measures, he should've quit trusting God by now. But he hadn't.

He still believed.

"I think Mack alerted us to something serious." Kane straightened to standing. "And it would've killed us if not for him throwing that rock."

Maria did the same, straightening beside him. Wanting to grab his hand so she could steady herself, but she couldn't rely on him any more than she already did. Kane Foster was more dangerous than a land mine any day.

She said, "Someone put a boundary around this location to keep people out. That means he's here. He has to be. Otherwise, why go to the trouble of making sure no one gets near it?"

Her father was here.

Kane grabbed her arm, and she realized she'd started moving. Going to her dad so she could have him back in her life. Finally, after so long.

"Let me go. He's here." She tried to tug her arm from his grasp.

He wasn't hurting her, but he also wasn't going to let go. "If he's in there, then getting killed because you made a run for it through a minefield isn't the ending either of you wants."

"There might've only been one. Who would go to the trouble of burying land mines all over this place?" She spread her arm, encompassing the trailhead where Mack had stood up and sweeping to the right. All the way past where Mitch was . . . "What is he doing?"

Their team leader swung his axe at a tree.

"His job?"

She frowned at Kane, about to speak when another explosion rocked the ground farther down the tree line.

Mitch stopped what he was doing. "Thanks, Mack. That was helpful."

Hammer dragged the kid back into a crouch. "Quit throwing stuff."

Maria heard Mack reply, but only caught ". . . see if there were any other . . ."

She figured he was trying to ascertain the extent of the problem.

Mitch went back to work on the tree, swinging the axe over and over.

"My dad could be in there." Maria clenched her fists by her sides. "He could be dying, and we're standing here."

The tree creaked and groaned, listing toward the trail. It toppled over and hit the ground, creating a single line between the trail and the tree line.

Nothing exploded.

"Sanchez—"

Whatever Kane wanted to say, she wasn't waiting around to hear it. Maria bolted down the trail, leapfrogged over Saxon, and raced for Hammer.

Someone yelled, "Get her!"

Hammer jumped up, reaching for her.

Maria leaped off the trail, out of reach, the way she'd done a hundred times in track and field. *Thank you, youth sports.* She landed with her toes on the fallen tree. She whirled her arms but caught her balance, then ran along the tree toward Mitch.

He moved to block her path.

When Maria slid off the end, he caught her. "Stop."

She caught him right back, clasping his elbows. "I have to know if he's in there."

"Even if it gets you or someone else killed?"

She looked him in the eyes. "I have to know."

"I know you do." He had an almost sad, understanding look on his face. "I know what it's like to worry over someone and not know what happened to them. Believe me, I know. But what I don't know is if you can follow orders when it really counts."

"Depends who is giving them."

"Hopefully I've earned that respect by now. Otherwise, we have no business being on the same team."

Maria let go of her boss, breathing hard. She stared through the trees and could make out a newer-looking cabin in the middle of a clearing. Not as nice as the cabins she and the boys had constructed during the offseason. They'd turned the Midnight Sun jump base from a derelict, forgotten military airfield that doubled as a base for the wildland firefighters—a couple of hangars and outbuildings and a stinky Quonset hut—into what it was now.

They'd spent all their pent-up winter energy fixing it up into a base for the hotshots, smokejumpers, and all the staff to live and work out of. A place they could enjoy and appreciate rather than turn up their noses at.

Maria was willing to concede that maybe Mitch had a point. They were supposed to be a team. "I worked alone for a long time."

Sure, she'd had a handler. When she'd made a call, someone on the other end had picked up to offer support. But at the end of the day, she'd been alone out there on missions. She'd faced her enemy solo and tried to slip out unnoticed. Which of course hadn't worked the one time she actually needed it to.

Cue, disaster.

The first friendly face she'd seen had been

Kane's. He'd walked into her cell dressed in camo, with paint on his face and a dark look in his eyes. On the way out of that desert compound, the truck had been hit with an RPG. They'd escaped, but in the confusion, Kane had been captured.

Because he'd come out to save her. Risked his life so she could have hers back.

The worst part was that he was *still* doing it.

Mitch said, "You aren't flying solo anymore."

Of course, it wasn't just the Trouble Boys who wanted to be part of her life now. The hotshots and their smokejumper friends were all in to figure out what was going on in Alaska with all these militia guys. Testing chemical compounds, using her father to create a substance they were going to deploy in the Midwest.

A senator had been captured in possession of one of several canisters, but that didn't mean it was over. There was still more out there, and they had to stop this impending attack. Only, the man who had it must've laid low to wait out all the attention, because there had been nothing since.

No sign of him or the substance.

Or her father.

Maria bit out a single word. "Fine."

Mitch said, "Good. Where's your axe? We're going to cut another tree to fall that way." He pointed through the trees, toward the cabin. "So you can go and find your father."

"Helping me get what I want is worse than telling me no."

Mitch chuckled. "It's called support. My wife said that's what women want."

Maria kept her expression impassive. "What women actually want is to borrow an axe and do it themselves."

He held it out, instructing her what tree to hit at what angle so it would fall in the right place. She had plenty of frustration built up in her, and he'd already downed one tree. Maria squeezed the axe handle and put all her strength into chopping the tree down as quick as possible.

Finally, it toppled over and hit the ground.

Mitch ducked into a crouch. She did the same beside him.

When nothing exploded, Maria said, "Maybe you should stay here."

Mitch frowned. "And why would I do that?"

"The aforementioned wife. Your kids. Pretty sure they want you to come home at the end of the season."

"They do. But that doesn't mean I'm going to let you go into this alone."

"That's why we're here." Kane hopped off the

tree, a thunderous look on his face, Saxon right behind him.

Hammer had a knife out and was carving something into a tree that hadn't been cut down.

The Trouble Boys didn't need any enhanced interrogation techniques. They had the silent treatment down like it was an art form. Those disapproving stares.

Maria wanted to spill the rest of her secrets.

But if her father really was in that cabin, she was going to get him out. When that was done, it would only be a matter of time before this was over.

She could keep her secrets. Kane would go back to his life.

Whatever they had?

It would be over before it ever began.

Sanchez might think fear was a tool to use, but it had only ever paralyzed Kane. Sent him right back to that night when he'd been locked in his seat by that belt, listening to Ridge cry. Staring at the back of their grandpa's head, frozen there, surrounded by darkness.

It didn't matter what the enemy threw at him now or anytime, or what had been done to him in Delta Force training to prepare him to face missions. Nothing in his life would ever feel like that moment.

Saxon grabbed his arm. "Don't kill her."

Two years and she still acted like she worked alone. But then, she could've walked away. They had made a pact to stick together because they were brothers, and that's what they did. She was supposed to be on board with it.

"Sanchez!"

She turned to look at him. "He's *my* father."

Kane's heart would've broken right then, hearing her say that. Her eyes so dark and sad he didn't know what to say. But his heart didn't break, because that organ had been shredded a long time ago.

Over the last two years, she had been slowly healing it, putting the thing back together.

And then breaking it all over again.

He managed to bite out the words "We go together."

She didn't like it, but she didn't move.

Kane made his way to her, where the clearing in front of the house didn't look like anyone had buried land mines all over it. In fact, if he had to guess, there was a spot to the right like an expansive lawn where a helicopter could land.

"Follow me. Step where I step, just in case."

"You really think there could be land mines here too? This close to the cabin?"

Behind the two of them, Saxon said, "Makes sense they'd be between the trail and the clearing, but it's still overkill."

"These people aren't known for their subtlety."

"And yet they've gone under the radar until now. This is a huge operation."

Saxon had a point. Kane said, "The senator should've spilled his guts by now, but he hasn't. So he's likely more scared of the guy in charge than he is of going to prison for the rest of his life."

Maria said, "He probably figures he'll mysteriously die in his cell if he talks."

Kane smiled slightly, because he actually thought her cynicism was cute. She'd been a CIA agent—cuter. In a stone-cold fox kinda way, as his grandpa would've said.

Something moved at the edge of his awareness. He stopped and tried to catch what it was.

Saxon said, "Two o'clock."

"I knew that." All of their instincts were attuned. They'd worked together long enough they could finish each other's sentences half the time, but that was weird, so they tried not to do it.

Sanchez touched the back of his arm. "We need to get to the house."

Kane scanned the trees over to the right, at their two o'clock. "It's an elk. He'll walk on, even if it isn't hunting season."

He stayed with Saxon and Sanchez, the three of them in single file in the middle of a clearing. Sanchez's fingers held on to his triceps. About as close as they were going to get.

The elk moved between two trees. Where a male would've had huge antlers stretching up from its head, this one didn't. A female.

Sanchez gasped. "There's a baby."

"Two of them." The calves both had brown fur with white spots on their hindquarters. They followed their mama through the trees and out of sight.

Sanchez squeezed his arm.

"Yep." Kane pulled his elbow forward so she had to let go. He got to the porch, and she hopped up beside him, going faster to the door.

"I've got the window." Saxon moved to the window right of the door, his gun in his hand.

Kane hadn't drawn his pistol. Anyone inside would've taken them out moments after they'd triggered those mines. An early warning system to whoever was inside.

"What do you see?" Kane used an Arabic word that meant "brother."

Saxon peered in the window. "Clear."

Kane tugged Sanchez back and squared up on the door. If it blew when it opened, he was the one who would be caught in the blast, not her. After all, he was already dead.

Unless she gave him a reason to live.

The door swung in so hard it hit the wall and bounced back. Leaves fluttered across the floor. One room, with a single door to a bathroom in the corner. Kitchen on the left. Cot on the right side that someone had used and not remade. Dust on everything, and a musty tang in the air. "Someone was here awhile."

Sanchez stepped into the cabin and wandered around. "Kept prisoner?"

Kane looked at the door again and the grooves in the wood. "Padlocked inside." With those mines . . . Why did his mind not want to lose the idea? "With an early warning system."

"The land mines? Whoever was inside would know if someone came near."

Kane wasn't so sure. "Or they're a way for someone who is elsewhere to know when a person approaches the cabin—or leaves it?"

"Then they rush over here and take care of the

problem?" Saxon came in, nearly as tall as the doorframe. "We should get out of here."

"We should look around and see if there's anything left behind that will help us." Sanchez put a hand on her hip but wasn't about to wait for permission.

Before he'd even formulated an argument, she turned to the cot and a stack of books beside the bed.

Kane looked at Saxon and mouthed, *Armed response team.*

Saxon tipped his head to the side and replied, mouthing, *Militia guys.* He actually looked excited for that possibility.

Land mines mean military gear.

Saxon mouthed, *We already know they're connected.*

"Are you guys done figuring out what their response will be?"

Kane glanced over at Sanchez, a smile pulling at his mouth. Of course she'd known they were talking while she looked around. "Find anything?"

Outside, someone whistled.

Saxon went to the door.

Kane moved to Sanchez's side. "What is it?"

"These books." She held one open, pencil writing in the margin. "This is my father's handwriting." She looked up, so much hope in her eyes. "He was here."

Those big brown eyes filled with tears.

Kane touched her cheek, running his thumb over it. No tears fell, but he could see she wanted to take a moment and grieve what they'd lost. What she'd been looking for since her father was taken from her.

Near as they could tell, the man had been traded like an asset. For years he'd been kept prisoner by criminals across the world. Hidden in dank places, forced to work for them until he outlived his usefulness and they traded him to someone else.

"We're going to find him." Kane shifted closer, wanting to take her in his arms. Not telling her something she didn't already know, but acknowledging that they both needed the reassurance. "We didn't come this far to quit when we're so close. We know he's nearby."

"But their operation was dismantled weeks ago. Where is he?" Finally, a single tear fell.

Kane wanted to draw her in and kiss her cheek. Wipe away the tear. He didn't, because that wasn't what was between them. And it couldn't ever be.

"Unless . . ."

"Don't do that to yourself."

She sniffed. "We don't know. He might have turned. He could be helping the last man because he's joined forces with them."

"Then why tell Dani about the fail-safe?"

"He could've escaped and made contact."

Kane shook his head. "That's why we're finding him, so we know for sure."

He didn't want to tell her that when her father had been in captivity for so long, he might've given up on being rescued. If it looked like he was working for these people, it could simply be that he felt as if he had no choice but to go along with it because he'd lost his hope.

She was about to speak when Saxon called out from the door. "Time to go."

Kane knew that tone well enough. He tugged on Sanchez's arm and moved toward the door with her. "What is—"

"Chopper inbound."

Sanchez still had the book. "It could be friendly."

"It isn't." Saxon ducked out the front door and onto the porch. "Get ready to run."

A split second later, automatic gunfire erupted in the distance, on the far side of the clearing. Bullets slammed into the porch, making a line of holes in the wood. Splinters kicked up. Saxon stumbled back, and Kane steadied his friend.

"Inside." Kane dragged both of them through the door and slammed it shut as more and more shots hammered into the porch.

He raced to the window and peered through the peeled-back corner of the yellowed film over the glass. A chopper crested the trees and lowered into view in the clearing, firing at them.

A second later, the glass shattered.

Kane fell back.

Sanchez screamed.

THREE

MARIA DROPPED TO HER KNEES beside Kane. He grabbed her arm. "Get down."

Thunder in his gaze.

Trying to protect her.

"You're the one who got shot. You stay down." She took the gun from the floor by his side and tucked it in her waistband. "Let me see."

The side of his shirt had a rip in it, soaked with blood.

He pushed at her hands. "It's just a graze. Don't worry about it."

Maria stared at him, then lifted the book she'd been holding. "Don't worry about it?"

His gaze flicked to the thick hardback, and she saw the moment he realized what she was saying.

The fact that the round had cut his side, then embedded itself in the book.

No wonder she'd been knocked back a step. She'd managed to catch herself before she went down.

"Don't worry about it, huh?" She turned the book so he could see the crumpled lead embedded in the cover.

He frowned. "Just stay down."

"Let me see it. You might need stitches." She laid the book down and started to lift his shirt.

"Don't." He shoved her hands away. "Saxon can look at it."

Maria just stared at him.

Saxon said, "Gunfire stopped." He moved to the side of the splintered window and whistled loudly.

A matching whistle replied from outside.

Kane sat up and moved away from her. As if that wasn't a giant "don't touch me" to her.

She'd noticed over the summer that he didn't remove his shirt when the other guys did, but this was the first time he'd rejected her touch.

Maria turned, still sitting on the floor, and looked at the room. Talk about being closer than they had been in months . . . or years, probably.

Her father had been here. He'd been held here. A captive.

This wasn't a retreat. It was a glorified prison cell.

Outside, the gunfire started again. She flinched and looked at the window, but nothing hit the cabin.

"They're aiming at the team," Kane said.

Saxon's head was bent to his task, his back to her so that she couldn't see Kane's side or how bad the wound was. "You'll live."

"No duh."

They'd shut her out, effectively. Not part of their team. Not privy to the things they knew.

After all that talk of being in this together, their fates intertwined and all that.

It was true, right up until they decided there was something she didn't need to know. Then all that solidarity talk went out the window.

Maria took the book—and Kane's gun—and headed for the front door.

She swung it open and stepped out right as Kane said, "Sanchez!"

Another dividing line—not calling her Maria. Trying to keep things professional.

She scanned the sky and found the source of the engine noise. The rotor. Military grade, private chopper. They'd already known these people were connected. That they had the kind of funding that meant they had far better equipment than the stuff the state and the Bureau of Land Management gave the hotshots.

She ducked her head and raced across the clearing, drawing the weapon. As if she was going to stand around in that cabin and let these bad guys shoot at her friends.

They'd already hit Kane.

Shot at her.

Someone could be dead already. And the fact no one had lost their life this summer almost made her drop to her knees and thank God for mercy.

Don't let it be my father.

She wanted to beg God, but that would be far too self-serving.

Kind of like asking for no land mines between her and a good spot to take a shot at that chopper.

She raced between the trees, weaving in and out. Finding the trail that elk had been wandering with her babies. Sprinting along it until she spotted the chopper overhead, the steady *rat-tat* pinning down the hotshots so there was nothing they could do but cover their heads and pray.

Running for it meant stepping on a land mine.

No way was she going to let that happen when she was the one who had brought them all out here.

Maria slowed to a stop, planted her feet, and held the gun in both hands. Aimed up between the branches of the spruce.

The shooter?

No, the tail. She inhaled, held her breath, and squeezed off a shot.

The helicopter listed to the side before the pilot corrected. The shooting stopped, and a second later, the chopper turned and flew away with the tail smoking.

Now they just had to get back on the trail and back to work. There was still a fire to deal with.

"No muss, no fuss, huh?" Hammer strode over to her, no humor in his eyes. His lips in a thin line. That impossibly square jaw softened by a thick growth of beard.

"Kane got shot."

Hammer flinched.

"Probably just a graze, but I wouldn't know because they didn't let me look at it." She didn't like that she sounded disgruntled, but how else was she supposed to feel about it? They'd shut her out. "How about you guys? Anyone hit?"

Hammer never gave much away in his expression. "Everyone is good."

"Great. No harm, no foul, then."

"And your father?"

"He was here, but he isn't here now." Maria strode past Hammer, heading for the fire road the hotshots had been walking on. Before Mack had thrown that rock. Before they'd approached this cabin. Before the helicopter. Before Kane had been shot.

She sniffed back the burn of tears, refusing to feel sorry for him when he clearly didn't want her sympathy.

Maria picked her way through the brush to the tree Mitch had directed her to cut down. Grizz and Mitch were crouched, deep in conversation. Mack and Raine huddled by another tree.

"Everyone good?" She walked the trunk like it was a balance beam. "Anyone hurt?"

Mitch shook his head. "We're good. I'm going to report in to Tucker about the mines and the chopper. I don't want anyone walking around when we have no idea if there are more mines."

She nodded, jumped off the trunk, and headed for Mack and Raine. "You guys okay?"

They stood together and made their way to the middle of the trail. Given the mines, it was probably one of the few safe places now that the chopper was gone.

Mack looked a little pale, but Raine nodded and said, "We're good."

Maria slung her arm around Mack's shoulders and tugged him over in a side hug. "Something to text your girl."

He laughed, but it sounded nervous.

"Maybe later though. When the urge to barf goes away."

"How'd you know?" He looked up at her, all dark eyes and dark hair. The kid was adorable but would never have made it in the world of international intrigue she'd lived in. Or in the military with his brother and the other Trouble Boys.

"I remember well enough my first few firefights. And I didn't have a team to back me up."

Raine said, "Did anyone see who it was on that chopper?"

Maria glanced around. Grizz just shook his head. Behind the burly mountain man, Mitch spoke into the radio, gesturing with one arm.

"I didn't. Not sure about Hammer."

"He jumped the berm and ran toward it." Mack shivered. "Maybe he saw something."

Grizz lifted his chin. "How about you guys?"

"No sign of my dad in the cabin, but he was

there. Kane was grazed but he said he's fine." She shrugged, as if it was no big deal. That was how Kane acted about it, so why couldn't she? "We should get to the fire. Aren't we supposed to put it out before it can jump the highway?"

She was ready to get this show on the road and all that. Do this teamwork thing she hadn't signed up for . . . while the guys shut her out and didn't let her help them.

Grizz snagged her elbow. "Not so fast, Sanchez. We need to talk."

She bit her lip where no one would see it.

He tugged her away from the rest of them, back the way they'd all come. "I'm sorry you didn't find your father."

She cleared her throat. "It's been fifteen years. Why would today be the day I got him back?"

"I know what it's like to lose people."

She wanted to shrug, but a thing like that wasn't something you brushed off.

"I know what it's like to wish you could've done more. But all you can do is the next right thing—while you pray that no one else gets hurt before this thing is over."

She lifted her chin. "I'm not here because I need help. I'm here because the world is in danger, and I'm the one who gets tasked with stopping the threat."

She managed to turn away before any tears spilled down her cheeks, then found her pack, tucking the book away but keeping Kane's gun handy.

Maria slung her pack on. "Let's go fight this fire."

"Dude, she is so mad at you." Grizz glanced over. "What did you do?"

Kane winced. "You don't want to know."

His side smarted, but it really was only a graze. The problem? Having Sanchez look at it—which would've been nice, actually—would've led to her seeing all the scars on his back. She knew they were there, but that didn't mean he wanted her to see them when he was hurt.

"Yeah, I do want to know."

Kane said, "It's complicated."

Grizz chuckled. "Pretty sure I said that to Dani. What I meant was that I didn't want to talk about it. Turned out she was right about everything. Not that she didn't have to change. We both did. God had us do the work to take those steps toward each other. Which might mean swallowing your pride and letting her in."

Kane just kept walking. Ignoring how his pack sat pretty much over the wound on his side. The pain reminded him of the risk inherent in all of this—and also, that he was alive.

"Thanks for the tip."

Grizz just chuckled. "I'd say enjoy the journey, but it's mostly frustrating until you admit to God that you have no idea what you're doing and you let Him lead."

He clapped Kane on the back and then jogged on up the line. Past Hammer, talking to Mack and Raine. Saxon was behind him, bringing up the rear.

He spotted Sanchez all the way up in front, talking to Mitch.

Kane glanced back at Saxon, wanting to talk but also not. He'd never been super verbal. It was much easier to figure out the thoughts in his head before he spoke aloud.

The same reason she'd run off after he'd shut her out.

Fresh on the heels of not finding her father, he'd pushed her away. Literally and figuratively.

All that mattered was that they'd saved her. He hadn't wanted her to know that the cost to get to her had been so high, but she'd found out pretty quickly. She knew what had happened to him, but neither of them needed the reminder of it right in their faces. Not when they were still so far from finishing this.

Grizz's advice to swallow his pride wasn't totally off base, but the guy didn't know how much they all had at stake in this. Sanchez had to focus.

All of them did.

Once she found her father, they found the canister, and this whole thing was done . . . then Kane would see what was left between them.

Mitch called out orders to cut a line and clear the brush from beside the highway while he and Hammer lit a backfire to starve the blaze of fuel.

The fire would be here within a few hours, driven this direction by the wind. When that happened, if the flames found nothing to consume, they would die out.

It was their job to make sure that happened. To draw a line. Here and no farther.

Kane heard a truck to the north. A cement truck rounded the corner in the distance and headed their way. "Car!"

Raine gave him an odd look.

"You didn't do that when you were a kid? You're playing in the street with your friends, and then a car comes and you all move to the sidewalk for a second?"

Raine said, "No."

"Well, what did you do when you were a kid?" She was one of the few Alaska natives on the team. Born and raised in Copper Mountain. "If you didn't hang out with your friends."

"I went to school. My mom worked, so I figured out how to make my own grilled cheese sandwiches." She swung her Pulaski at the ground and dragged it through the tangled roots that would provide a network the fire would travel along unseen.

The cement truck buzzed past, riffling his hair and flapping his shirt against the wound on his side. Even through the bandage it smarted.

Up the shoulder of the highway, Sanchez watched him.

He lifted two fingers. She turned away and went back to her task.

Saxon dug his shovel in the dirt. "Keep trying. Maybe one day she'll forgive you."

Kane wanted to argue, but he wanted her to forgive him. Not that he thought he'd done something wrong. It was up to him who saw his scars.

"Hammer has his own reasons for wanting to come across as invincible."

Kane glanced over at Saxon. "Says the guy who walked away from a plane crash."

Raine said, "Actually, I think he was carrying Neil."

Saxon rolled his shoulders. "All part of the job, ma'am."

Raine shook her head. "You macho guys."

"Admit you feel safer with us around."

Raine said, "Only I after I point out that there were no run-ins with gunmen, helicopters, and absolutely no land mines before you guys showed up." She held up one hand. "I'm just saying."

Kane glanced at Saxon. "She might have a valid point."

"That's the stuff that makes life fun."

Raine shot an odd look at Saxon and went back to her work.

Kane swung his Pulaski, ignoring the pain in his side.

"Just answer one question for me," Raine said. "If these guys have one canister of this stuff ready to go, can't they go ahead with the plan? Why has nothing happened?"

Kane said, "You want them to destroy crops in the Lower 48 and ruin the US economy? I'd rather we stop the person behind this and whoever is funding them."

"Right. But I'm saying, it's been a couple of weeks. Whoever has that can . . . what are they waiting for?" She shrugged.

Saxon jumped on his shovel, driving it into the dirt. "Who knows why? Could just be they're waiting for the heat to die down. I'm just glad it's giving us time to keep working the problem."

Kane had been thinking about that last night, sitting on the hill. Trying to keep his thoughts from straying to Sanchez. "I think it's that fail-safe. The one Dani told us that Sanchez's father mentioned."

"Isn't that what would stop it from going off?" Raine asked.

"Sure. But if Sanchez's father told these guys that there's a code he has to enter or something like that, then they'd need the code before they could use it. So maybe having the canister isn't enough."

"That would mean they don't have her dad to give them the code," Saxon said. "Or he refuses."

"Either way."

Saxon said, "Either way, we still have no idea why they haven't set it off yet. The FBI is on the case, and Alaska State Troopers. Everyone is looking for the guy who has the canister, and we have no idea who it is."

Kane glanced over, shooting his friend a look. One Saxon would understand. Because maybe they *did* know who it was that had the canister.

Raine said, "Who is he, anyway?"

Kane was going to have to lie. Again. About something else.

One day he was going to crack and just start telling everyone the truth about everything. Who cared about the fallout? And there definitely would be plenty of destruction.

Especially when Sanchez found out he loved her.

Cue explosion.

"Guys?"

Saxon said, "We aren't sure."

Which only meant they had an idea. But Kane had more than an idea.

He'd seen the guy with his own eyes weeks ago and hadn't believed it then. But now that they knew Jeremiah Redding had been involved in this, it was clear his whole family would be too. That meant Elias.

After all, an operation like this? It had the Redding family written all over it. Chinese funding. The economy at stake. Money laundering through foundations like the Northern Lights Higher Education Fund. A massive operation that involved dirty Feds and illegal land grabs, secret compounds and the dangerous testing of chemical compounds.

Yeah, they'd seen it all before.

But that'd been halfway across the world and several years ago.

This? It was practically in their backyard.

And it stank of Elias Redding. They all knew it was him—most especially after his cousin had been here in Alaska just weeks ago. Jeremiah was dead, so of course Elias had come to clean up—or continue the mission.

Their former teammate.

Their brother. Their friend.

The teammate who had betrayed them.

Now it was up to them to make sure he didn't betray this country.

FOUR

SOON AS THE HOTSHOTS SHOWED up back at the base camp, Tucker pulled them all into a briefing about the chopper and the cabin. The smokejumpers, Tristan, and Jamie were there, along with Dani and Crispin.

Seemed like everyone on the Midnight Sun crew—along with their significant others—was invested in the outcome of this one.

After Maria took a shower, most everyone had already gone over to the mess hall to eat. She found an Adirondack in front of the firepit and sat, staring at the charred wood under the grate.

The base dog wandered over and curled up by her leg, his chin on her tennis shoe. She reached down and scratched his head. "Hi, Jubal."

His tail wagged, but he didn't move otherwise.

She sat back and looked at the sky. How many times had she done this with her parents? Laid out bedrolls under the stars. Now she had an app that told her what all the constellations were. As if she needed someone to tell her. But she used it anyway to find their favorites.

Even if it meant sitting out here the rest of the night, until dark fell. Or what passed for dark up here in the summer.

"Not hungry?" Raine slumped into the chair beside her, eyeing the dog. Eating a protein bar. The girl thought wings were gourmet, and going out for pizza was the highlight of her monthly budget. But Raine was all backcountry, and there was no other hotshot female Maria wanted to fight a fire with.

"I'll get something later. When the line dies down."

Raine snorted. "Right. Anyone that thinks Kane is the broody one isn't paying enough attention."

"No one needs to pay me attention. That's the point."

"Is that what you use your super-secret spy skills for?"

Maria looked around. "You're not supposed to say that word out loud. I told you in confidence."

"Relax. No one is out here with us."

Raine had no concept of surveillance technology, but that was probably a good thing. She had no need to hide her thoughts or her feelings either, usually.

Still, despite being able to read her, Maria was convinced Raine was hiding something. Probably just paranoia, but she hadn't been able to let go of the fact this woman had a secret. Maybe a dark one.

It just didn't have anything to do with international security, terrorism, or people trying to destroy the US and start a war. Likely, it was a lot closer to home.

Kind of like everything else right now.

"So, your father was in that cabin?" Raine chomped down a huge bite of her protein bar.

"At some point. Might've been last week, and it might've been months ago."

"But you're close."

Maria said, "Not close enough that I know he's safe. He might as well be on the other side of the world."

"Why is it that the people we don't want anything to do with seem like they're always around and the people we want in our lives are out of reach?"

Maria glanced over. Raine watched the sky where a tiny plane disappeared into the clouds, a wistful look on her face.

"Want to talk about it?" Maria asked.

Raine scrunched up her nose. "JoJo told me to pray about it. Give my fears and my dreams to God. I don't know if it did anything."

"It's been fifteen years since I saw my father. Maybe I'm kidding myself that he hasn't gone over to work for these people."

Just thinking about those books in the cabin made her remember all the times they'd talked about stories. Or read old Jules Verne classics together. They'd talked about codes embedded in verse, and it had sparked her learning how to decode messages.

The CIA had found her on an online forum where she'd cracked a code they'd created just to see if anyone could break it.

She'd been recruited before she even finished college.

All of her skills were things her father had taught her growing up. So much of who he was, the man who had raised her, was embedded in this operation. The canisters. The tests. The numbers Jamie had copied onto the mess-hall map at the beginning of the season.

How could he not have turned? He was obviously helping them.

"Maybe I'm just trying to find my father because he's the one who masterminded this whole thing and I need to be the one that saves the world from him." Maria didn't like saying it out loud, but if she couldn't be completely honest with Raine, then who could she talk to?

The guys had been great, but she would always be one step removed from them. Just the woman their team protected. The asset.

Raine considered her a friend. A sister, of sorts.

"Dani said she saw your dad on his knees with a gun to his head. You think he turned after that?"

Maria shrugged.

"You want me to tell you to keep the faith? To never give up hope that he's a good guy, or that in fifteen years he's never wavered? Never done anything but fight the people who have been trading him around like a commodity?"

"Of course he's wavered," Maria said. "Anyone would have."

"You know what it's like to be a captive. So maybe just hang on until you can hear the truth from his lips. None of us does the right thing every single time, and he's been living under extreme stress for years."

Maria couldn't catch what Raine wasn't saying, but she could hear it in her tone. There was more. Raine's own hang-ups, maybe. "It feels like he's still as far away as he always was. Even if everyone keeps saying we're closer than we've ever been."

She'd even tried to convince herself that was true.

"Just don't go off on your own, okay?"

Maria glanced over.

"Tell someone first. If you're gonna leave the team for him."

"I'll tell you. Okay?"

Raine said, "I'll hold you to that."

"If you answer a question."

"Here it comes. The super spy and her interrogation tactics trying to get me to spill."

Maria laughed. "If that was going to work, I'd already know everything there was to know about you by now."

Raine grinned. "Go ahead, then. Do your worst."

As if that's what this was. "Why don't I just ask, and you can decide if you trust me enough to answer?"

"Where's the fun in that?"

Maria said, "I'll call Tristan. Have him come over and ask."

Raine gasped. "You wouldn't dare."

But there was more to it. This wasn't a woman with a crush and no other cares in the world to speak of. The undercurrent was far darker, but Maria didn't know what could have possibly happened between Tristan and Raine.

It wasn't like they'd spent much time together, even if Tristan had been around the last couple of weeks—since he and Crew had both burned their association with the Sons of Revolution militia group. The ones who had been running around the backcountry, shooting at wildland firefighters.

Maria could ask her friend plenty of questions. But bringing up Tristan shut everything down. She stared at Raine, deciding to give the other woman a break from talking about Tristan. "Why did you become a hotshot?"

"So I could escape them."

"Who?"

"All of them."

Maria shifted in the seat, dislodging Jubal. "Sorry, dog." She petted his head, and he found another place to lie down. "Talk to me, Raine."

The other woman scrunched up her nose and shook her head. "Doesn't matter now. I'm a hotshot. I don't have a family. I only have this." She motioned at the jump base around them. "I don't need anyone to feel sorry for me. It is what it is."

Her friend, this strong woman forged by the savagery of the Alaska landscape, had become a hotshot to escape. Maria said, "I only became a spy to be privy to any intel on my father. The government considered him a threat for years until they realized he was being trafficked for his scientific skills. Sold to the highest bidder for what he could do. And they only know that because I dropped proof they couldn't ignore on their desks. I've been trying to get him back."

"They didn't help you?"

Maria snorted. "The CIA tried a couple of times to 'buy' him like a sting operation. It never worked, and I'm half convinced they'd have locked him away in some kind of facility where he'd be no better off than he is now."

"So you've gotta bust him out!" Raine sat forward on the chair, tossing her wrapper in the firepit. "Like Tristan did with Crew."

Maria frowned. "Turns out I have to find him first. Remember?"

"Oh yeah." Raine sat back in the chair with a sigh.

"Our shot at getting inside intel dried up when Crew and Tristan were discovered."

Raine winced. "I, uh . . . actually might have a way to find out what you need."

"That one." Kane put an X on the map on the wall in the mess hall. The one Jamie had listed numbers in the corner of months ago, back when they'd had no idea what it all meant.

No idea what was going on in this part of Alaska.

They'd been through kidnappings, a plane crash, met up with dirty federal agents, backwoods thugs, revolutionaries. They'd destroyed a whole facility, kept these militia guys on the run for weeks, and now finally had a shot at exposing the entire operation—taking down Senator Deville.

And yet this thing was far from over.

Rio, an FBI Special Agent out of Anchorage who had a personal connection to the smokejumper team, came over, scratching his jaw. "You're sure?"

Kane said, "Ask Mitch. We were all there."

"We're sure." Grizz settled on the edge of the table.

Rio looked at the clock. "When are the smokejumpers due back?"

"Probably tomorrow," Grizz said. "They're fighting the south fork, and the wind is too strong for the chopper to pick them up tonight."

Mitch sat across a table from Mack, eating chili. The rest of them had finished already. Kane's mouth was still on fire from the spices, but he wasn't going to admit that. He was just going to keep drinking water.

A table over, Logan and Jamie sat close. Logan had been grounded after passing out during a jump a couple of days ago, so his team had deployed without him. Jamie's brother Tristan was across the table from them, beside Crew. The two men were confidential informants for the Feds, as far as Kane could tell.

Actually, he wasn't sure what Tristan was. Some kind of career undercover guy, or a Fed who'd been burned when his handler turned out to be dirty. Either way, it was too close to what had happened to their team.

Crew had been recruited as a confidential informant for the Feds because he could get in with the militia without being suspected.

Now that the Sons of Revolution knew who Tristan and Crew were, they had no way to go back in undercover.

"What?" Rio lifted his chin.

Kane said, "Just seems like this place collects misfits. People who don't want to be remembered and can't have their name on a roster anywhere else."

"You boys just happened to choose firefighting?"

Saxon wandered over and punched Kane in the shoulder, not that it had much strength to it. "We don't like to sit around."

"I don't suppose you'd be doing the fate of the world any favors if you did go sit in a safe house and let the Feds take care of this guy with his canister."

Kane grinned. "Exactly." Plus, they'd all go stir crazy in a safe house. He couldn't even imagine Hammer, Mack, Saxon, him, and Sanchez in close quarters like that. Out here, they got to work. They could fight back the force of nature in all its destructive glory, protecting both people and their property. "Wildland firefighting isn't so different from the Army."

Rio chuckled. "The fate of the world does seem to follow you guys around . . . and Sanchez. She was Army too?"

Saxon said, "No comment."

Rio frowned. "I'm not a reporter."

"They've already briefed Dani on not asking questions." Grizz folded his arms across his chest.

Grizz had been in the Army for a while and knew exactly what kind of team the Trouble Boys had been on. He knew enough not to talk about it, and he'd told Dani not to ask or do any poking around online. Not that she would find anything.

"If she wants an exposé," Saxon said, "she can pester Crispin into talking about who *he* is."

Rio chuckled. "Good luck getting him to spill."

Kane figured Dani would be disappointed when she couldn't do a human-interest story on the team. Thankfully, she'd been distracted by the aftermath of Senator Deville's arrest and the fact that there was still a canister out there.

Rio said, "So we have nothing on Sanchez's father at that location?"

Kane pointed at his penciled X on the map. "This one was a bust, even if we know he was there at one point." He stared at the map, wanting to pace up and down so he could figure out where they needed to look next.

Eventually, they would run out of places Sanchez's father could be hiding.

A plate shattered, and then a thud. "Logan!"

Kane spun to find Jamie crouched beside

Logan, who lay on the floor. Tristan rushed around the table. "We need help!"

Hammer and Mitch went to them.

Kane couldn't get close because of the crowd of hotshots and their friends and family. Mitch and Hammer lifted Logan between them, his arms over their shoulders.

Mitch said, "Let's get him to the med bay. Have the doctor come check him out." The hotshot boss didn't look happy.

Mack followed them. Tristan and Jamie, who swiped tears from her cheeks. Dani came over to Grizz, who put his arm around her.

Saxon said, "Wilson?"

Kane recalled their buddy in Delta Force. A guy who'd suffered too many blows to the head and been discharged with a traumatic brain injury. He nodded. "The doc will know for sure."

"You think it's a TBI?" Rio glanced at the door where the others had gone out. "I saw him nearly pass out a few days ago."

Grizz said, "That would fit his symptoms. He's been knocked out more than once this summer. Maybe something worse is going on?"

Dani glanced around, still tucked under Grizz's arm. "Where is Sanchez? Or Raine, for that matter. I haven't seen them."

Kane had been purposely trying not to think about her. "They didn't come over."

Saxon cleared his throat. "I saw them by the fire."

But he hadn't said anything, because even though Kane wanted to know . . . telling him was far too much like giving an addict what they wanted. It wasn't what was best for them.

He went to the map. "What have our militia friends, the Sons of Revolution, been up to since the senator was arrested?"

"Seems like they've dispersed," Rio said, "but I'm not getting anywhere near the intel I was getting before. The compounds we knew of have been abandoned. Their website indicates they're still actively recruiting."

Kane turned his back to the wall and folded his arms across his chest. "We need a few days of good rain so we can take the time to search all these locations rather than just looking at whatever is closest to where we're being deployed."

He never would've said that if Mitch or their commander, Tucker, had been in the room. Everyone here had to put the fires first. But with national security on the line? This was more than finding Sanchez's father.

Kane looked at Rio. "Is the FBI going to find the canister before it's deployed?"

The guy looked sick. Considering the fate of thousands could be on the line, as well as the country's economy, Kane didn't blame Rio for being nauseous. Rio said, "I have another issue. There's a new player here, though I haven't identified him yet, and I think the canister changed hands." He shifted and pulled out his phone. "Intel indicated a trade was being made. We thought it might've been Sanchez's father, since they mentioned 'the doctor,' but no one showed up."

"It was a ruse?" Saxon asked.

Rio shrugged. "We might never know. Could've been finding out how much *we* know. Testing our response. Things have been too quiet. It makes no sense."

"Because what are they waiting for?" Grizz said. "Why not just use it now?"

Rio said, "Let's thank God for His mercy that they haven't. Okay?"

Kane nodded. "Your intel says the canister is still here, right?" When Rio nodded, he continued. "The longer it's here, the more people will be closing in on them. Why wait?"

"They think all of you are done looking. That it ended with the press conference." Rio glanced at

Dani. "Our idea worked. They've got all the time in the world as far as they're concerned."

"Okay, that's scary."

Kane was inclined to agree with Dani. "Means they've got plenty of time to plan it out, be calculated. They won't rush and make mistakes."

"But it also means we have more of a chance to stop it," Saxon said.

Kane heard the echo of the door out in the entryway. A second later, Sanchez pushed through the interior door. Her eyes scanned the room and found him.

He'd already pushed off the wall and started toward her. "What is it?"

"Just an idea."

Saxon was right behind him.

"Care to share?" Rio said from behind Saxon.

Kane lifted his brows. She caught the expression and glanced at Rio saying, "I'm not sure the FBI needs to be involved. Until there's evidence, or at least probable cause."

"Right." Rio huffed a laugh. "Don't ask, don't tell?"

Sanchez smiled.

Kane said, "We'll keep you posted."

"Sure you will." Rio lifted his hands. "So as not to incriminate myself, I'll be going back to work.

That way when I have to arrest you guys later, I'll be able to deny all knowledge."

Grizz and Dani followed him out.

Kane called out after them. "Text me when you know something about Logan."

Grizz waved a hand over his shoulder. The guy probably didn't want Dani in any more danger than she'd been in already this summer.

"What is it?" he asked Sanchez.

"I can get into a party. It's a place to look for my father—and this canister. But it has to be tonight, and you guys can't come inside. It's by invite only."

"Overwatch?" Saxon asked.

Sanchez nodded.

"How did you get an invite?"

Kane had been about to ask the same question. Was he really going to do this? Just blindly follow wherever she led them in the search for her father? Let himself be swept along by her determination to find him and stop this?

Never mind.

Of course he was.

It didn't matter where Maria Sanchez went. He would always follow.

FIVE

MARIA GOT OUT OF THE CAR AND eased the skirt down. "Who knew you had something like this in your wardrobe?"

Raine pocketed her keys in a tiny purse. "You never know when you're going to need to blend in at a high-society party."

Maria looked at the mansion Raine had driven them to. It certainly was a high-society place. A vacation home for the rich and famous who didn't like the warmth of the Lower 48 in summer. Still, not the kind of place she wanted to live in, even if she were ever able to afford it.

She didn't glance back but knew Kane and Saxon were parked in a truck down the street. Nearby enough that they could help out if either she or Raine indicated through their comms that they needed help. But not so close they'd be picked out as watching the house.

In fact, she wasn't sure she wanted to think about Kane at all.

Far better to focus on the task at hand, the way she'd compartmentalized in the CIA. As an officer, she'd undertaken all sorts of missions. Regardless of whether they'd been part of her personal mission to find her father, she'd worked them to the best of her ability.

Between the comms earbuds and the tracker rings they wore, there wasn't much more they could do make sure they were safe.

"Can you hear me?" Kane's voice in her ear wasn't her choice.

"I copy you."

At the same time, Raine said, "Got you loud and clear, Saxon."

Rather than all four of them on one channel, which would be hard to distinguish, they'd opted for two channels so everyone could focus.

"Be safe," Kane said.

"We're just going to look around." She didn't need to rush in, guns blazing. The CIA had trained her to deal with situations with a lot more finesse than Delta Force—and with a lot less backup. "Besides, I'm not the one who got shot today."

Raine glanced over at her, a smile tugging her lips.

Maria ignored the comms and said to her friend, "How did you get us invited, anyway? You really just made a call?"

She was a local. It stood to reason she had contacts.

"There's someone here I need to talk to," Raine said. "So I won't get in your way."

A tall guy in a tuxedo stood at the front door, one hand clasping his other wrist. She spotted a gold watch and noticed he wore an earbud, a clear wire disappearing beneath his collar. "Good evening, ladies." He seemed to recognize Raine. "How are you this evening?"

"Well, thank you." Raine handed over her purse, and the man looked inside.

Maria didn't fuss about doing the same, but only because he wouldn't know that her things weren't the inconspicuous items he'd think they were with one glance. When he handed her purse back, she smiled. "Thank you."

He opened the door for them. "Have a good evening."

Maria smiled, following Raine into the house.

Inside was at least ten degrees warmer than outside and smelled like coconut. The hum of people talking filled the air, and through an open arch, she spotted people all over, dressed in high-society party attire. A whole lot of suits and tuxes, tight dresses, and clinking glasses.

Someone moved, and she spotted a roaring fireplace, which explained the warmth.

She'd been a firefighter too long, because Sanchez would rather be sitting out under the stars, spending the night sleeping on the ground and eating MREs, than making small talk with the kind of people who filled this house.

She flicked her freshly curled hair off her shoulder and smoothed down the side of her dress.

"Raine!" An older guy in a suit with no tie strode over, one hand in his pocket. In the other hand, he had a short glass with amber-colored liquid, a ring on his index finger. His gaze moved through Maria and dismissed her.

Which was the idea.

Raine stepped into his embrace and held him for a second. "Happy Birthday, Grandpa."

The older man chuckled. "You make it sound like I'm ancient."

"As if you couldn't still out-hunt me any day."

"You better have your tags ready for the fall. I've got it all planned."

"I bought a new scope for my rifle." Raine grinned. "I've got it all sighted in."

The older man chuckled. He let go of Raine and put out his hand. "Robert Howards. Good to meet you."

"You too. I'm Sarah." She had used the name often in the CIA as a cover. It slipped out now without her even thinking it through. "Happy Birthday, sir. It's good to meet you, though I had no idea this was a birthday party."

He kissed the back of her hand. "Don't tell anyone it is."

Maria smiled. "I should freshen up. Could you point me to the restroom?"

Raine actually looked relieved. She probably wanted a moment alone with her grandfather, given the house was packed with people.

"Down the hall to the right." He pointed over his shoulder.

Maria wandered that direction, sauntering as if she had all the time in the world and was as relaxed as she could be at a party for the evening. Inside was far different. Her thoughts warred in her head, and she pushed them all back.

Her father might be here and he might not.

She would only know for sure by looking, so what was the point of wondering herself to death? She needed intel. Access to a computer. She needed to clone a phone and do a room-by-room search of the house. All things she'd done in the CIA.

But Kane hadn't seen any of that. He only knew the officer who'd been captured and held for weeks. He knew the woman who'd failed and needed rescue.

It stood to reason he wouldn't need her to help him when he was hurt. That he felt as if he always needed to be the strong one.

"Did you do that a lot in the CIA?" he asked in her ear. "Excuse yourself to go to the bathroom and then sneak around?"

She glanced both ways down the hall, then said quietly, "It's a classic for a reason."

He chuckled, and it sounded warm.

She didn't want to like it. She didn't want to need him with her or rely on him. After all, when this was over and he didn't need to protect her, he'd go back to his life. She would be left to figure out why she hadn't been able to keep it professional. Why she'd let him break her heart.

But she would have her father.

Finally.

Fifteen years of searching, and it would all be over.

Maria found the restroom. She kept going down the hall, snuck into an empty office. Raine's grandfather's office. "I can't believe she didn't tell me."

"What?"

She glanced at the door, moving to the computer on the desk. "Raine didn't mention her grandfather or his birthday. She *said* she could get me somewhere I'd be able to get intel on the canister. Did she lie, or has she known more than she said this entire time?"

"Either way, it doesn't look good for her," Kane said. "Saxon is transcribing their conversation. It's just small talk so far."

"Do we know who he is, this guy Robert Howards?"

"I sent the information to Jamie, but who knows when she'll be able to look him up? Rio sent me a text. Logan was transported to the hospital. They might keep him overnight for tests."

Maria winced and crouched, finding the ports for the computer. She pulled the lipstick from her purse, unscrewed the bottom, and inserted the flash drive into the USB slot. It would immediately start copying every file on the hard drive. "I hope he's okay."

"Whether he is or not, he'll have all of us there to help him. And his family from Last Chance County. They'll show up, I know they will."

Right. Because that's where he'd grown up. "Guess you know them all."

She looked around the office for a file cabinet or a safe. There wasn't much she could do if the lock was high tech, as she didn't have all her equipment.

Hopefully, copying the hard drive would get them information.

"I've been gone a long time," he said. "I doubt most of them even remember me now."

She doubted that. As if Kane Foster was all that forgettable. Or was it more about them currently believing he was dead?

Once in a while, she entertained the fleeting dream that he might take her home with him and introduce her to his family, as if he was proud to have her with him. As if she was worth trusting.

Worth loving.

But the dream never lasted long. Reality always intruded sooner or later, and she realized it was impossible. He'd have let her in by now if he was going to.

The door handle turned.

"Someone's coming." She crouched and ducked under the desk as the door opened all the way.

"Empty. Like I said."

"Good," a second person responded. "Because the helicopter with Elias will be here in five minutes, and I don't want anything upsetting him."

Everything inside Maria solidified like she'd been doused with ice water.

She squeezed her eyes shut and saw him in her mind.

Her nightmare. The man who'd shown up when she was captive in Syria was here. *Elias Redding.*

The man who had betrayed them all.

"What is it, Sanchez?" She'd gone silent. Kane bounced his knee in the truck, determined not to get out and run into that house. The woman was going to drive him crazy not letting him know what was going on. "What's happening?"

She'd better not be in danger.

More likely she just couldn't tell him and he'd have to wait. Be patient. *Lord, teach me quick.* Eventually she'd be able to talk out loud.

He should text her.

Kane leaned back so he could drag the phone from his jeans pocket, ready to send her a message.

"They're gone," she whispered.

"What happened?"

"They just looked around, then left."

He frowned. "That's it?"

Beside him, Saxon glanced over. "Bro, you need to chill. She knows what she's doing."

Kane shot him a look. *I'm fine.*

"Ask her if she can find out why Raine's comms went down."

Kane ignored his friend and spoke into the comms. "Any way you can check on Raine?"

Sanchez came back, "Is she in danger?"

He relayed the question to Saxon, who shook his head. "We don't think so."

"Then it can wait."

"Why?" Kane frowned. "What's going on?"

"There's a chopper coming in. I'm going to use the distraction to finish looking around the house. See if my father is here. Or if he's *been* here."

He didn't like her tone. Sounded like she wasn't saying everything. "Did you copy the computer files?"

"It just finished." She was on the move. "I'm looking around."

Kane said a prayer for Logan, who was in the

hospital having tests done. Everyone was worried about him. Logan's family in Last Chance County were finding out he was under the weather. After Kane had prayed for them as well, he prayed for a way that they could figure this out without Jamie having to worry right now or step away from Logan's bedside to help them.

They needed a break—a way to end this.

No more searching or running down leads or ideas for leads. Just results.

He scrubbed his hands over his face.

Saxon tapped his shoulder. "Chopper."

Kane said, "Any idea who's on it?"

Sanchez didn't answer. She probably couldn't risk talking aloud right now. Saxon grabbed a pair of binoculars and zoomed in on the inbound aircraft. His buddy said, "Who knew our little Raine was part of all this?"

"Can't choose your family," Kane said. "She hasn't left the base in weeks except to fight a fire. Maybe she only did now because we needed a lead."

"I don't like that her comms are down. Seems like she might've shut them off."

"She probably just wanted a private word with her grandfather." Kane wasn't going to worry until there was a reason to. "Wanna stay here?

I'll sneak closer, check out the helicopter and who is arriving."

Saxon shrugged. "I'll reboot and try to connect with Raine."

Kane pushed the door open and closed it quietly.

In his ear, Sanchez said, "You should stay with the truck. It might not be safe."

He raced across the street and snuck around a house. "Safe is relative, isn't it?"

None of these mansions had backyards. What they did have were exterior lights and motion sensors, so he'd have to be careful.

"I mean it, Kane." She sounded serious now. Maybe even worried about him. "Stay in the truck. I've got this handled."

Kane eased past the neighbor's patio and ducked behind a hot tub with a good view of the backyard. She was really shutting him out? "We're gonna need to talk about this."

"No, we don't—Oh, hi. Didn't see you there." She giggled.

Kane frowned. He'd never heard her make that sound.

"Just talking to myself. Don't mind me."

The back door opened, and she stepped onto the lit patio. Strings of fairy lights had been hung in the trusses of a covered porch. A chef at the far side worked the outdoor kitchen, and Kane had to admit the scent of citrus and chicken smelled amazing.

A man followed her onto the porch, taking her arm.

"Let go of me."

He was close enough to her that Kane heard him say, "Don't think I will. You're going to explain why you're wandering all over Mr. Howards's house."

"Well I never. Treating me like this." She morphed into some kind of high-society snooty . . .

Kane thought it was cute. As long as he wasn't the one who had to deal with that drama. He switched his comms to the channel where he'd be able to hear both sets of earpieces. "Saxon, anything from Raine?"

"Not yet."

The guy manhandling Sanchez dragged her around the side of the house, behind a little storage shed that was nicer than the house he'd grown up in. He shoved her up against the wall behind it.

Kane had to get out from this spot before someone saw him creeping around and called the local sheriff. And he had no intention of leaving her with this guy.

"Who are you, and why are you at this party?"

Sanchez cowered a little, but not much. She wasn't so good at acting helpless. Not really in her nature. "None of your business . . . and because I go wherever I want."

Kane raced between the houses.

As he approached the guy's back, she whipped out one hand and jabbed it into the guy's throat. He choked and started to go down.

Kane caught him and laid the guy behind the shed, where no one would easily see him. Tucked away in the shadows.

"I didn't ask for an assist."

He got his first close-up look at her outfit and nearly swallowed his tongue. Tall heels. A skin-tight black dress. Every curve he'd been ignoring for two years seemed to shimmer in the light. And she'd done something to her hair that left it wavy and loose.

Sanchez set a hand on her hip. "Like what you see?"

Before he could rewire even two brain cells, she spoke again.

"Looking for some of this?" She waved at the guy she'd throat punched.

He fought back the raging fire and said, "We should get Raine and get out of here."

"You're the one who needs to leave, Kane."

She might as well have tossed a bucket of ice water over his head. "I'm your backup, remember?"

"There's a chopper coming. You shouldn't be here when it gets here." She motioned to that dress again. "I'm the one who blends in."

She didn't seem to understand how much attention she drew. The woman was a knockout, as Grandpa would say.

"Raine is off comms. We need to go. You've already been discovered, and any other security will be looking for you . . . and this guy." He wanted to take her arm, but it would probably feel too much like that guy manhandling her. "Can we go? Please?"

She looked over his shoulder, up into the sky.

Wind kicked up, ruffling his hair and flapping his jacket against his sides. The sound of the inbound chopper had been a low rumble, but it was much louder now. Kane glanced over his shoulder and saw it slow as it lowered toward the ground.

She wrapped her fingers around his arm, just above his elbow. Her very cold fingers. "I need to see who is on the chopper, but you don't. Two of us run more risk of being seen than one."

He turned to her, stepping close. Shielding her

from the wind. "Why are you trying to push me away?"

She lifted her chin. With her face upturned, he could see brown in her eyes where in shadow they would look almost black. "I'm not pushing you away. You got hurt today."

So she was protecting him?

Was that it?

"I don't need you to look after me."

Indecision flickered in her gaze. "That isn't . . . we should just go. This whole thing might've been a bust, but I have the flash drive. I copied files from the computer, but if it's Raine's grandfather's, I don't know what it could have on it."

"Yeah, we need to talk to her about that. She dropped a bomb on us, and for what?"

Her attention shifted over his shoulder.

She touched his arm again, holding on like she needed solidarity. He started to turn to look at the chopper so he could see who was getting out.

"Kane—"

He had never heard that tone from her before.

She tugged on his arm, drawing him back to face her. But where at least part of him had been expecting to see affection or even that she might draw him close and kiss him, that wasn't what he saw. She was trying to distract him. Because she didn't want him to see who'd climbed out of that chopper.

"What are you doing?"

She winced. "Don't look. Just give me your gun. I'll take care of it."

Kane reached back and clasped the butt of his gun, drawing it from his waistband. "Saxon, Redding is here."

She grabbed a handful of his jacket. "Give me the gun, Kane. I'm going to kill him."

SIX

WE'RE NOT KILLING HIM." KANE held on to her, holding her back.

Maria let him. "Why not?"

She already had what she'd come for. All she needed to do was get the guys out of here before they were discovered. Before the unconscious man on the ground woke up and sounded the alarm, or one of his buddies came looking for him.

Kane didn't even look over his shoulder. If he did, he would probably be the one determined to kill Elias Redding.

Their enemy.

The man who had betrayed the Trouble Boys, who was responsible for her being captured, and who had hurt Kane so badly just because he could, stepped off the helicopter like this was a social visit.

"We aren't going to kill him," Kane said, his tone tight. "If he's here, it's because he's involved in this situation. He'll know where to find your father and that canister."

"He's our shot at ending this."

"That's why we need him alive."

Maria nodded. "Good."

Kane frowned. "What?"

"When you want to kill him, remember that." She grabbed his elbow and tugged him away, toward the front of the house. "Tell Saxon we're leaving."

No one else had disembarked that chopper. Her father wasn't on it.

"Your dad isn't here?" He sounded genuinely disappointed.

"I have a copy of Howards's hard drive. We might be able to get something from it. Find out why the canister hasn't been deployed yet."

"Because they need a code." Kane walked with her toward the front yard. "Because they need your dad to make more since we got all the rest."

Maria frowned. "If they need more, why not just steal it from evidence? I doubt it's been destroyed. That wouldn't happen until after a trial."

Kane said, "Sax, did you get that?"

Maria switched channels on her comms in time to hear Saxon say, "I'll call Rio."

She said, "We need to find Raine. Elias Redding can't see us here, or he'll recognize us and we'll never get our hands on the canister. They'll disappear, and I'll never find my father."

Kane squeezed her hand, then didn't let go of it. "We didn't come this far to give up now." Those words had become their mantra—the code they'd lived by since they were declared dead. After a second pause, he said, "Raine shut off her comms, but we can go in the front again and find her."

"I'll go. One of us will draw less attention than both."

"You don't need to protect me from him."

"I'm protecting all of us."

Kane didn't respond to that. But then, she didn't need him to, did she. After this long, she knew what he was thinking.

As much as she might want to tear through that house and search every inch of it for her father, she would have known if he were here. For such a high-value asset as her father, there would have been way more armed guards in the house. She'd seen it in other places, when she'd come close to finding her father before.

"I'll go get Raine." She tugged on her hand, but Kane didn't let go.

"Be careful."

"I'm better at this than fighting fires."

He smiled. "I believe you. I'll be out here praying."

Maria bit her lip because he knew how she felt about God. She went to the front door, and the bouncer guy let her in, but not before she gave him a twenty-dollar bill.

In the front entryway, she scanned the crowd for Raine and spotted her friend over by a bar that had been set up in the corner by the pool table.

She caught Raine's attention and motioned with her head.

The other woman said something to her grandfather and kissed his cheek before wandering over. "What is it?"

"I need to go. And so do the guys."

"My grandfather was just about to introduce me to someone."

"He isn't the kind of guy you want to know."

Raine tugged a folded paper from her purse. "Like the kind who would give me a note for you?"

Maria unfolded it and found a handwritten note, unaddressed and unsigned.

>JM>I'm sorry. I'm going to fix everything.

"Who gave this to you?"

Raine said, "If we need to go, then we need to go."

Maria heard Saxon in her ear and told Raine, "Turn your comms back on."

Raine said, "I needed to have a private conversation." But she reached up and switched it back on.

"Did you have it?"

The other woman nodded.

"Then it's time to go."

The commotion at the other end of the room was swelling, and Raine's grandfather looked around—probably looking for Raine.

In her ear, Saxon said, "Rio is on his way here. The FBI is going to raid the house."

Raine turned back to the room.

Maria shoved her to the door. "We're already on our way out."

"Hurry." That was Kane.

"What's going on?" Raine followed her through the front door.

Maria waited until they were out of earshot of the bouncer, then said, "I think you know exactly why the Feds might show up here. Don't you?"

Kane met up with them by the fountain and walked behind them down the long drive.

"I don't know what you're talking about." Raine's plea didn't have much strength to it. Probably because she'd known they weren't going to believe her before she'd even said it. After all, she was the one who'd brought them here—precisely because she knew her family was connected.

Which meant there was a whole lot Raine hadn't said. Even if she tried to live like she knew nothing and had no connection to this situation, it was a lie.

In her ear, Saxon said, "Two minutes. I'll pick you guys up out front."

Maria said, "Why don't we hang around, and you can tell Rio that you have no information?"

Raine whirled around and faced her, forcing Maria to stop walking. She said, "I'm not part of it."

"But you were prepared to do the right thing and bring me here."

"So you could look for your father!"

Maria eyed her friend, understanding how she might want to hide her connection to a group of dangerous people. How some might consider her untrustworthy because of her family.

"I know what it feels like to be judged for who

your family is." Maria had been forced to train harder, score higher, and prove herself over and over because her father had been suspected of voluntarily working for criminals all over the world. As if he would have orchestrated his wife's murder and left Maria just to get paid.

No way.

"I know what it feels like to have to prove who you are. To wish you could be judged on your own merit, not maligned because of something someone else did."

Raine's eyes filled with tears. As she shook her head, the moisture glistened in the light. "You don't know anything about me."

Saxon pulled up at the curb in his 4Runner. Kane opened the back door right as a commotion erupted on the street. Screeching tires. Men in dark fatigues and helmets, carrying assault rifles, raced across the grass, coming out of every corner, every shadow, the white FBI letters on their vests prominently visible in the dark.

A tactical truck pulled up to the curb, followed by three other SUVs. Another two SUVs came from the other direction, and personnel poured out of all of them.

"Stay where you are!" It was Rio, striding across the lawn to the front door.

The bouncer had run inside.

One of the agents rammed the door open, and they all raced inside.

Raine sucked in a breath.

"Will your grandfather comply, or will he fight them?"

She shook her head, and a tear fell.

"Who gave you the note for me?"

Kane said, "What note?"

She would show him later, but right now she needed information. And she needed to get the copied hard drive somewhere the FBI wasn't going to find it in her possession.

Raine said, "Grandfather gave it to me. He said he was glad you came, and that he'd been asked to give it to you."

"We should get in the car and go." Kane looked around. "I'm not waiting around for Elias to see us."

They all ducked into the SUV, and Saxon drove down the street. He weaved around the FBI vehicles, ignoring when he was flagged down to stop.

Saxon nodded to the agent, then hit the gas and sped away. "We've got bigger problems than the FBI being mad at us if Elias is here."

"He'll be in custody by tonight."

Kane sounded like he almost believed that.

Maria glanced at Raine on the other side of the back seat, then said to the two guys in front, "You think he isn't able to dodge FBI custody? He hasn't come this far to get snatched up by the Feds with no way to get free. Rio won't know how he ties into it, so he'll just talk his way out of it."

What they needed was to come back and follow Elias to see where he went. Surely he would lead them to the canister. A guy like that wasn't going to leave it to someone else to carry out the plan.

That had to be why he'd come here himself.

Kane figured Sanchez was right enough about that. No way would Elias end up in a jail cell tonight.

But there was a risk *they* might.

Or at least that Rio might not share any more information with them. Probably they'd be shut out of the investigation from here on out.

Not that it mattered.

Far as he knew, dead people couldn't be confidential informants.

Saxon pulled onto the highway. He had that edge to him he got sometimes—usually when there was a traitor nearby. Or when he was about to flip things around and take a stand.

Kane shifted far enough in the seat that he could draw his weapon, hoping he didn't need it for whatever was about to happen.

Half a mile later, on a quiet stretch of winding highway, Saxon hit the brakes and pulled over.

He got out, so Kane did the same.

Saxon opened the back door and tugged out Raine.

She sputtered and yelped, but Kane knew Saxon had no intention of hurting her.

Saxon walked her to the back of the SUV and backed her up to the rear door. "Talk."

"Or what?" Raine yelled. "Are you going to drag me around some more? Or walk me into those woods and shoot me in the head?"

She didn't seem scared of them, but she was hiding something.

Sanchez left her door open. "Is there a reason we couldn't do this back at the base?"

She sounded tired. He wanted to make sure she got sleep tonight, as they'd no doubt get deployed to fight a fire first thing in the morning. But that was the besotted guy talking. Not the operator on a mission.

Even the team guy with a woman he was protecting would ensure they all got enough rest. But that kind of guy wasn't the one who'd passed up becoming a smokejumper when he'd wanted to—because he knew he could do it. And that he'd like it.

No, the guy who'd stuck with the hotshots again this season had done it for more than just to be around so she was protected.

Saxon folded his arms across his chest. "Talk."

"I'm not involved with the militia." Raine sniffed. "I have nothing to do with them or anything they're doing."

"But you know them," Kane said.

Sanchez shifted. As attuned to her as Kane was, he could tell she wanted to ask a question. But she wouldn't want her friend to think she was targeting her, going on the offensive. Burning their friendship for the sake of the mission.

Raine said, "I wanted to help. That's all. I didn't have to take you there tonight, and I was risking plenty bringing you there to look for your father."

Saxon said, "Why would you believe he was there?"

"Look." Raine brushed hair back from her face. "I didn't know if he was there. I just . . . I didn't want to go by myself, okay?"

Sanchez said, "You could've just told me you wanted a wingman. Or a bodyguard."

"I know you guys are all about your mission. You don't need to get involved in mine."

Kane frowned.

"What mission?" Saxon asked.

Raine shook her head. "It doesn't matter."

"You can trust us." Sanchez eased closer to Kane, standing beside him, shoulder to shoulder.

He wanted to take her hand.

But like everything about their relationship, it wasn't the time.

"Don't worry about it," Raine said. "You guys are, like . . . saving the world and stuff."

"We'll help you as well, if we can. You should know that." Saxon had that warm tone the ladies liked, but Raine didn't seem to respond to it.

She just sniffed. "I went to the party to ask my grandfather a question. I got an answer. It isn't good, but why would I have expected something different?" She shrugged. "Go figure. So now you know. This is my life." She waved her arms, encompassing the tall pines on both sides of the highway.

No cars. Nothing but an empty road. The scent of fire on the breeze. An orange glow on the mountain to the north, and the sun almost to the horizon even though it was after midnight.

"What did you go there to ask him?" Kane knew Saxon wasn't going to let this go until he had an answer.

Raine looked away, shaking her head.

Sanchez said, "You know we're the good guys. You think we're too busy to help you, but we know how to multitask. You've seen it."

"I've been living it for months," Raine said, the edge of a smile on her lips. She glanced at Sanchez. "Every fire we go fight, you guys are looking for Sanchez's dad. Or looking for bad guys to fight. Searching for intel. Trying to save the world."

"Hiding." Kane had caught the edge of something in her tone and wondered if he could draw it out of her. "Laying low up here in the backcountry. Pretending we aren't who we really are, because if anyone found out, then we wouldn't get to do what we need to do."

Raine said, "I need to fight fire. I know it isn't enough for you guys. It's just a distraction. But this is what I love. It's who I am."

Kane nodded. "We get it. No one is going to mess this up for you. But we need to know why you went to that party."

It hadn't been simply to wish her grandfather a happy birthday.

Nor did Kane believe she had anything to do with what was happening.

Raine swiped at her cheeks. "I needed to talk to his second-in-command. My grandfather's lieutenant."

Sounded like they were military. Or Mafia.

"I needed to know who killed my father."

Sanchez flinched. "Someone killed your dad?"

Kane reached over and grabbed her hand, holding on to it so she had an anchor. She needed the Lord to be her firm foundation. But if Kane could help, then that had to be part of why God had put him in her life.

Raine said, "He wasn't even a good guy. He never treated my mom right, and she hated him until the day she died. But he was my father." Her voice broke. Raine cleared her throat. "My grandfather isn't going to be around much longer. When he's gone, I won't have anyone."

"I'm so sorry." Sanchez gave Raine a hug.

When she stepped back, Kane said, "Did you find out who killed him?"

Raine nodded. "But it won't do me any good. Even if my grandfather said I should tell him where to find the guy so he can kill him. It isn't going to bring my father back. And having him in my life never did me any good anyway."

Kane said, "I know what it's like to love someone but not like them. Loyalty is loyalty. But it still breaks your heart."

Sanchez glanced at him.

No, he'd never told her about his mom and dad. In fact, there were a lot of things he hadn't told her. After all, it wasn't like she needed to know when none of it was pertinent to the mission at hand.

But the longer things went on, the more he found himself wanting to tell her.

Wanting to show her who he was.

"I don't know what I'm going to do. But I know it's not as important as what you're doing," Raine said. "Can we go back to base now?"

Kane looked at Saxon.

The guy didn't seem appeased but moved for the driver's door. "Let's go."

Raine got in behind him.

Kane held the door for Sanchez. She stopped before getting in, holding him with that steady gaze. The one that made him want to tell her everything.

"Maybe you can share that story sometime."

Kane said, "Maybe." Far as he could see, they

were a little preoccupied with finding a canister and stopping a terror attack. "Elias is here."

She nodded. "That means they needed the big guns. Someone to get this done."

"Agreed." He nodded. "Now all we have to do is figure out how to stop it without anyone getting caught in the crossfire."

Sanchez lifted up on her toes and planted a kiss on his cheek. "Thanks, Kane."

She slid into the seat, and he shut the door. For the moment he was alone on the highway, he allowed himself a smile. Just that one acknowledgment that, for a split second, he'd had it all.

Everything he wanted.

But duty always came first. The mission, and Sanchez's search for her father, would always be a higher priority for both of them.

Maybe it just wasn't meant to be, and God wanted to teach him how to let go.

How to let the Lord be in control of the future.

"Just don't make it a painful lesson."

Kane wasn't sure his heart could take much more.

SEVEN

MARIA SAT ON THE SIDE OF THE bed, lacing up her boots. She'd had about half an hour of sleep between their operation last night, wondering about her father, and looking at the computer.

She'd loaded the files from Robert Howards's computer onto her laptop as soon as they got back to the base, but knowing he was Raine's grandfather put a different spin on it. She'd never undertaken a mission where the target was someone she knew—or their relative.

Her dad wasn't a target—as much as some at the CIA wanted to believe otherwise. He was a victim.

"Ready?" Kane stood in the doorway.

"Did the smokejumpers leave already? I heard

the plane take off." She finished lacing her other boot.

"That was them. Hammer is covering for Logan since he's still in the hospital, but the doctor cleared Orion, so he's good to go. Orion is back on the team as of today."

She stood. "I sent Jamie an email, but unless she wants to distract herself from what's happening, she might not look at it. What's the latest with Logan?"

"Still undergoing tests." Kane backed up from the doorway, and she came out, her pack over her shoulder. "Ridge, my cousin in Last Chance County, said Bryce is on his way up here. He's Logan's twin."

He didn't often talk about his cousin—unless they were alone. "Ridge works on the same vehicle as Bryce at the fire department, right?"

Kane nodded, looking a little pleased. Because she'd remembered?

"It's not that hard to keep from forgetting details. It's not a spy thing."

Kane smiled, about to say something. But that was the gateway to things getting personal, which was the last thing either of them needed.

"We're late." Maria waved for him to go ahead. "Let's go."

Raine walked out of her room and hurried past them, looking like she'd had about as much sleep as Maria.

Kane and Maria followed her through the living area of the women's cabin, out onto the porch.

The runway lay east to west, at a slight angle, in front of them. Mess hall and hangars on the far side. Office to the right. RV parking to the left.

She dug the note from her pocket and handed it over as they crossed the grass to the office.

Kane unfolded it and read, "'I'm sorry. I'm going to fix everything.'"

"It's his handwriting." She had the book from that cabin yesterday. "I know it is."

She wasn't going to look at the compassion—the pity—on Kane's face. She didn't want to see it. Not when everyone who learned what had happened to her felt that way. Until they decided they agreed with the assessment that her dad had somehow planned the attack that'd killed her mother and left Maria orphaned, for all intents and purposes.

"Between that note and the computer files I had to wade through . . ."

"You didn't get much sleep."

But she didn't want to talk about that. "Why

didn't you take Logan's place on the smokejumper team? I know you can do it."

He glanced over. "I love skydiving."

"So why not sign up for it? Saxon would still be on the hotshot team with me. And besides, I don't actually need babysitters." He'd buy that, right? She didn't like the idea that she'd held him back.

That he'd chosen to give up what he loved because of her.

"You should've gone for it."

"Because you'd have gone for it too?"

He had offered to teach her in the offseason so that she could have easily passed smokejumper training.

Maria said, "Just because one of us does something, doesn't mean the other has to do it too."

"I'm not protecting you if I'm miles away, fighting a different part of the fire."

Maria didn't even know why she was pushing this right now. But she couldn't let it go. Things weren't better, not for all the trying they'd done. All the months of searching. Fighting militia guys. Looking all over the area for her dad. Nothing had changed.

Maybe she needed it to.

"I'm picking a fight with you." Because he wouldn't leave, no matter what. She knew it, but that didn't mean she should actively push him away.

"Ask the question." He turned at the door to face her, stopping her from going inside.

Closing her in, like he did. Forcing her to make a decision. To stick with him—because she had to admit that was what she wanted.

"I want to tell you the answer."

Maria wasn't sure she wanted to hear it. Especially not when he looked at her with those green eyes and that brooding stare.

"Ask me."

Maria swallowed. "Why aren't you a smokejumper?" He should be one. He would be amazing at it.

"Because you're afraid of heights."

She gasped. "You weren't supposed to know."

He tugged her around so her back was to the wall and stepped close to her. "You think I didn't notice? I notice everything, Maria."

She bit her lip.

This morning had taken a turn. It was out of control.

Was she dreaming? This was awfully close to some dreams she'd had. Where he closed that gap between them, his body pressed up against hers, and he kissed her.

Like he'd always wanted to.

Like he wanted nothing else.

"If you're scared, I want to know." His face lowered, far too close.

She could smell the mint on his breath.

"I'm not afraid."

The corner of his mouth curled up. Oh boy. They were in dangerous territory.

She should've told him that she had no idea what she was doing. Between the CIA and the hunt for her father, she hadn't had much time for dating. Except that one inkling of a . . . Yeah, that had been a disaster.

Someone cleared their throat.

Maria looked around Kane's shoulder. "Mack!" Her voice was far too loud. "Good morning."

Kane chuckled, but he didn't step back. She squeezed out from between the building and his body and pulled the door open like this was completely normal.

Mack's cheeks flared pink. "For some more than others."

She was going to kill Kane. "I think we're late for the briefing." She took the stairs, jogging up like she normally did.

Mack raced her, and they stepped out into the

upstairs hall, laughing. Flushed, which was good because no one would think it was about Kane.

Rio stood in the far corner, talking to Mitch and Tucker. Why was the FBI at their morning briefing? The rest of the hotshots were here, Grizz and Saxon talking. They were only missing Hammer, who'd gone out with the smokejumpers. Raine was over by the window, looking out at something or someone outside.

"All right, everyone." Tucker clicked his remote, and the screen lit with a map of the area. "There's a big storm coming in tonight with the potential for lightning. So we're expecting fire activity to increase over the next few days. As such, Rio is here to update you all on the ongoing investigation. That way you'll know the Feds are taking care of their business, and you can all take care of yours. Namely, fighting fire."

Kane handed Maria a mug of black coffee and settled into the seat beside her.

"As you may know"—Rio shot them a pointed look—"we made a number of arrests last night. But no dice on the canister or the man we ID'd as the guy who first escaped with it. Or your father, Sanchez. Sorry."

She nodded.

Rio continued. "We're questioning Robert

Howards, but he seems to have few direct ties to these people. At least, not ones we can present to a judge."

Maria glanced at Raine.

Kane said, "How's that possible, considering who he had at his house?"

Raine glanced over. "It was a birthday party."

In the light of day, it didn't look like she was so inclined to trust them. Someone had killed Raine's father. Maria could certainly understand not wanting to drag anyone else into it.

If her dad had been killed instead of just being missing? Maria wasn't sure she wanted to think about how far she would go to get justice. Question was, who would be the target of Raine's vengeance?

"We also brought in Elias Redding last night for questioning. Though apparently, he had only arrived by helicopter a short time before. We have no idea where he was coming from."

"How does he know Robert Howards?" Maria figured they had to be connected. Why else would Elias have shown up to the party?

"They're business associates." Rio glanced around. "Unless anyone here has information they'd like to share with the FBI about the nature of their relationship?"

Raine glanced at Maria. Maria said nothing. Even Mack seemed to know something was up, but he'd probably heard the guys talking last night after they got back. Still, the kid kept his mouth shut.

"That's what I thought," Rio said. "I've got to get back to Anchorage after I check in with Crew and Tristan."

Raine stiffened in her chair.

What was that reaction about?

Mitch said, "Crew is gassing up the bus. He's going to drive these guys to the fire. Not sure about Tristan."

"Got it." Rio headed for the door.

"We all good?" Tucker asked. "No one itching to go solo, save the world?"

Alone was just asking for trouble.

No one said anything, but only because whatever they did, it would happen as a team.

"Great. Have a safe day."

Nine hours later—not that Kane was counting—they loaded back onto the bus. All of them were covered in sweat and completely exhausted. Kane should've been hungry, but they'd had

MREs for lunch, and those things had enough calories to keep an elephant going for three days.

Mack slumped into a seat, lying down with his knees on the end of the seat and his feet in the aisle. "Someone wake me when we get back to the base."

Saxon kicked the kid's foot. "Sure, but you won't like how I do it."

Mack groaned.

Grizz sat up front with Mitch. Raine tucked into the row right behind them.

Maria climbed on the bus last, her hair damp at the hairline and whisps plastered to her face. Tired, but the good kind that meant you'd done a long day of good work. The kind that saved lives, even if it only felt like digging a trench.

For a second he thought she wasn't going to sit near him, but she came over and took the seat behind his.

Kane turned and put his back to the wall, his legs on the seat.

Saxon did the same across the aisle, facing him, but looked at Maria. "You good?"

She leaned back on the seat and closed her eyes. "So tired."

Kane smiled. "I dunno. I could go for a run when we get back."

Saxon grinned. "Four miles. No, let's go for six."

Kane chuckled.

She and Mack both groaned. Mack said, "My feet hurt just thinking about it."

Maria opened her eyes and pinned Kane with a stare. "You aren't really going to go on a run, are you?"

"Am I a smokejumper?" If she didn't go, it wasn't happening.

Saxon said, "Whatever that means."

But it didn't need to make sense to the rest of them. It only mattered to her.

She said, "I'm afraid I have a date."

Kane stiffened. When had she made time to—"A date?"

"Yes, with a pizza and my pajamas."

Saxon laughed under his breath.

"Right," Kane said. "Pizza sounds good."

"I'd invite you, but I'm probably going to eat half a slice and then fall asleep."

He returned her smile. "Fair enough."

Saxon turned to the window, where the land arced up away from the road so that it seemed to crest like a wave above their heads.

Mack looked like he'd already fallen asleep.

Kane turned in his seat to face her. Not as close

as he wanted to be—like outside the office this morning. But he'd settle for this.

He knew he'd pushed it a little. He wanted to get under her skin, so why hold back? But it didn't help either of them focus on what they were here to do. "How are you doing?"

She leaned forward, pressed her forehead against the seat, and turned her head so he could see her cheek. So she could say "I can't stop thinking about him" and only he would hear it. "Whether he's scared. If he's running for his life, or if they've got him locked down so he can't go anywhere."

"I know what that feels like." Kane shut his mouth. Why had he said that?

She scrambled his brain—especially when she was this close.

"I've been praying for him," he said, trying to change the subject away from him knowing what fear felt like.

She lifted her head. He should've known she wouldn't let it pass. "Do you mean when you were captured in Syria?"

He didn't think about that and certainly never talked about it, so he didn't have to lie. Because that wasn't what he'd been referring to. "It happened when I was a kid."

She frowned. "What did?"

Kane had to take a breath. He didn't want to talk about it, but if it helped her, he would. "We were riding in the car with our grandpa, my cousin Ridge and I. Our moms are sisters, and Gramps was the only grandparent we had worth anything. He used to take us to baseball games, and we'd get hotdogs."

The memory made him shiver, even though it never really got fully dark up here. That was a small mercy he'd thanked God for.

"We were driving home, and it was late. He had a heart attack." Kane cleared his throat.

"Oh no!" She whispered it, but it still seemed far too loud. Only because he rarely told anyone this.

"The car went off the side of the road into a ditch. He died, and I broke my leg. Ridge broke his collar bone. We couldn't move. We were stuck in the car, and Grandpa was dead." He sucked in a breath. "The Last Chance County rescue squad showed up and cut us out of the car, so when I say I know what it feels like to be helpless, I mean it. I know."

She laid her hand on his arm and nodded. "I can't imagine that. I'm so sorry you lost him."

"He was the best." He smiled. "Ridge and I

made a pact to always do what Gramps would've been proud of."

"So you joined the Army."

"And he became a firefighter. The same crew that cut us out."

She squeezed his arm.

"I'm praying for your dad. I know you don't believe but—"

She cut him off. "You do, and there's power in that."

"Gramps expected us to go to church. Eventually it stuck, then after it was a habit, I started actually listening. I found what I'd been missing. Hope. Peace. For an angry teenage boy, that counted for a lot."

"Sometimes I feel like my life stopped that day," she said.

She didn't talk about the day her father had been captured much, and spoke of her mother even less. "Tell me what happened."

She rubbed her nose. "We were in New York. At a symposium for scientific research into . . . something. I don't remember what it was. We walked out of the front onto the sidewalk and . . . all of a sudden there was so much noise. Squealing tires and shouting. It sounded a lot like that FBI raid last night, but it wasn't cops. All these guys just ran over to us, and my dad yelled and got in someone's face. Trying to protect us. One of them shot my mother." Her eyes filled with tears. "Right in front of me. She just . . . fell down. Dad was yelling at all the men like he didn't even realize she was dead. I ran to her, and I didn't see what happened. A door slammed, and all the tires squealed again. He was gone. She was dead on the sidewalk."

Kane reached over the back of the seat and touched her cheek. "I'm sorry you lost her."

"The police called my aunt in Boston. I lived with her for a year, then went to college. But it wasn't really living. I was only going through the motions." She winced. "Maybe I've been doing that ever since."

And if she opened up her heart to the Lord, or to Kane, she would have to feel again.

Kane's heart squeezed in his chest. *Lord, keep her heart safe.* If it was a choice between not having her in his life the way he really wanted, or watching her have to grieve everything she'd lost, he wasn't sure he could ask her to fall in love with him.

"Heads up." Saxon shifted on his seat. "Crew!"

Mack moaned on his seat.

"I see them," Crew yelled back. "Everyone buckle up."

Maria said, "This thing doesn't have seatbelts. What is it?"

Kane could see out the back window. "Two trucks, and they're coming up fast behind us."

Before he'd even finished telling her, the first truck rammed into the back of the school bus.

They swerved on the road. Mack rolled off the seat and scrambled back up. "What's happening?"

"Keep your head down," Saxon told him.

The truck came at them again.

Mitch yelled, "I'm calling the sheriff. Everyone hang tight."

"He won't get here in time." Kane dug in his pack and pulled out his gun.

Saxon did the same. "Plan?"

"I'm thinking." Mostly about using the emergency door at the back and jumping from a moving school bus onto the hood of a truck.

Or, you know, just firing some warning shots.

"Think fast," Maria said. "Before I do."

He didn't like the sound of that. The CIA came up with some off-the-wall ideas sometimes.

The truck hit them again, followed by the second vehicle.

The bus swerved across the highway, where a semi headed toward them.

"Hold on!" Crew dragged the wheel back the other way.

Kane's body pressed against the window. He held on to the seat and his gun.

The bus bumped off the side of the road and down an incline. It went airborne for a second before bouncing down, throwing them all out of their seats.

The bus listed over and hit the ground on its side.

Kane shook off the daze, not knowing how long he'd been out for. Being unconscious, that night in the dark with Ridge fresh in his mind, wasn't good. He was liable to panic.

Someone stepped on his hand. Mack lay across his legs, blood on his temple.

"Hey—"

The butt of a gun slammed into his head, but not with enough force to knock him out right away.

He was awake long enough to see two guys lift Maria and take her.

Before he could do anything, the whole world went black.

EIGHT

MARIA WAS ABOUT READY TO QUIT pretending she was unconscious.

No one was saying anything, and there were at least two other people in this room with her. A room that smelled musty and damp and maybe like it had been used to store hay or soil at some point.

Now she was in here, tied to a wooden chair. Feet secured to the legs, hands tied to the sides by her hips.

Her head hurt from the bus crash that had shaken up everyone. Elias Redding—who she wanted to call every nasty name she could think of—had hopped on the bus like it wasn't flipped on its side and dragged her away.

She was surprised he hadn't killed everyone else

on the bus but wasn't going to ask him why not. Didn't want the mess of multiple murders on his hands? Maybe he still felt some kind of brotherhood connection to the guys even though he was their enemy now.

Whatever it was, her mind would rather wonder about that than focus on the fact she had no way out of this chair or this room and no idea what was about to happen.

"Maria."

He knew she was awake.

She lifted her chin, blinking so her eyes could focus. Single bare bulb with a weak yellow light. Elias and another guy in a cargo jacket—one of those militia people. And another man, standing in the shadows in the corner. Wearing a suit.

Not good.

Especially given the tray of what looked like surgical instruments on the rolling cart to one side.

She said, "I've seen this TV show."

Now playing the part of Sydney Bristow . . .

Hmm. How did that intrepid double-agent spy get out of the predicaments she found herself in? Maria could use some of that information right now. A way out. A lifeline.

It started with getting out of this chair.

Elias stepped forward. "I think you hit your head. You're not making any sense, Maria. But you need to start talking, or this is going to take a long time. And it'll be painful for you."

"I think your mother probably dropped you when you were a baby. I mean, normal people don't do the things you've done." Did he really think she was going to cower? It hadn't happened last time, so why would she have changed? If anything, she was stronger now than she'd been two years ago.

Elias slapped her cheek with an open palm. Her face whipped to the side, her skin burning.

Maria blew out a breath. "This feels familiar, *Elias*."

"It should. Seems like you and I are destined to go around and around."

"So just tell me what you want, I'll tell you what I know, and we can get this thing resolved." She lifted her chin. There were far too many guys in here for her to make a stand and try to escape. She couldn't fight all three tied to a chair, and she also couldn't find out what they wanted if they left the room and she escaped.

Elias chuckled. "Very well. Give me the code to deploy the canister."

She bit her lip. Not what she'd expected him to

say, and she couldn't react to it. Otherwise, he'd know she had no clue what he was talking about.

But now she knew why they were alive.

They had something he wanted, and Elias couldn't kill them until he got it. Which made Maria leverage. Her father, leverage. Her friends, leverage. They were all weak because they cared about each other enough that they'd refuse to let the other get hurt if they could do anything about it.

She pretended to consider his request. "Hmm, let me think about . . . no."

Maria wanted to adjust this awkward position on the chair, but she was tied so tightly she couldn't move. She managed to wiggle her fingers, curling her right hand enough to know she still wore the ring.

One of Jade's tracker rings.

Which meant her friends—her Trouble Boys—would find her.

Elias tugged something from his back. A phone. He took a picture of her, the flash so bright the white spot stayed in her vision after he was done.

"Kane isn't going to make a trade with you," she said.

"You think I care about him right now? That's

a loose end for later. Don't worry. Those guys will get what's coming to them for betraying me."

"Betraying you . . ." She nearly choked.

"Your father, however? He's the one who will show up for you. Isn't that right? Wherever he's hiding, he'll burrow out and trade your life for the code. So it really doesn't matter if you tell me or not. Either way, I'll get what I want."

Her cheek burned where he'd slapped her, but that was nothing compared to how it felt realizing he was going to play the victim. Elias seemed to have convinced himself that he was in the right.

Probably thought destroying America was some kind of righteous cause. A way to fix everything that was broken.

Her father was gone. "Hiding?"

Elias said, "Don't play coy. He's probably contacted you by now and your Fed friends have him in a safe house, all cozy."

"Probably."

He'd sent her that note, but it hadn't been for them to meet up. In fact, it had sounded more like her father didn't want her to find him. That he was going to do what he needed to do, and she should stay out of it.

As if she would *ever* give up trying to find him.

"Tell me the code and we can forgo all the back and forth." Elias stood over her.

She had to look up to see his face, making pain shoot through her head. She winced, because she wanted him to know that she was in pain, and eased out a breath between gritted teeth. "You think I'm going to tell you anything?"

She kind of wanted her dad to show up to rescue her. That would actually be nice, considering how long she'd been trying to do that for him. Once in a while, it felt good to be the one being rescued.

Not that she planned to be here long enough that her boys had to go to the trouble of getting her out of this situation.

"Don't worry. You will tell us." Elias walked to the door.

His buddy held it open, and the two of them walked out, leaving her alone with the man in the shadows. And the instrument tray.

Definite Sydney Bristow vibes.

He stepped out of the shadows, and Maria realized why Crew, Tristan, and Special Agent Parker had been talking about these guys being connected to the Chinese.

"You look like a fun guy," she said, trying to keep her tone light. "I can tell."

He stared at her, his face almost gaunt. Dark eyes full of shadows. "Your father thought so."

Breath caught in her throat.

She wasn't going to pray just because she was scared that she would suffer before she got out of this situation. Or that she might not get out of it at all. Maria wouldn't be the person who reacted because their back was against the wall. She needed a plan.

She could use some help though—she wasn't unaware of that. The Trouble Boys had rescued her last time, when Elias and that group of militants had held her prisoner in Syria. Kane probably hadn't stopped praying since the bus. If he was alive, or conscious. *Please be okay.* She had no idea who was hurt and how badly. Her friends. Her teammates. The man she wanted to . . .

No, don't think about that.

Otherwise, her last moments would be about regret.

The man stepped toward her, holding a pair of pliers. "This is most likely going to hurt a great deal."

She stared at him. "Bring it on."

It was the only way she knew of to beat the fear. Stare it in the face and not back down, because that meant giving in, and if there was one thing her father's life had taught her, it was that you didn't lose heart no matter what happened. No matter how long it took to get out of a horrible situation.

I'm going to fix everything.

Maria tipped the chair to one side, then the other, rocking a little so she could test the sturdiness of the frame.

He closed in, reaching for her index finger. "Hold still, dear."

Maria screamed in his face. As soon as she had the chance, she would make her move.

Or she would die trying.

"*Paging Doctor Weston.*"

Kane sucked in a breath and sat up on the hospital bed. "Saxon!"

He was in a tiny bay, curtains all around him. The light-blue material whipped back, sounding like a shower curtain rail. But it wasn't Saxon, it was Crew. And Tristan was right behind him.

"Report." Kane didn't have the authority to demand it, but he didn't care. How long had he been out? Long enough they'd all been transported here. Who knew what condition everyone was in? And Maria . . .

She'd been taken.

Crew stood at the end of the bed. "Okay, take it easy."

Kane started to argue.

Tristan said, "Do you want to know the situation or what?"

Kane held his tongue.

"Good," Crew said. "Grizz, Mitch, and Raine are fine. Just bruises. Mack regained consciousness, and he's texting. The smokejumpers are too far into dense wood on treacherous terrain. They can't be airlifted out. Hammer said to 'do what you need to do'—whatever that means."

Kane nodded.

"Okay, fair enough." Crew sighed. "Saxon is getting his arm stitched. It was cut on the edge of the seat."

"Thanks." Hopefully it wasn't bad, because he needed his buddy for this. "What about finding Maria?"

Crew said, "Tucker has the password to the system that will locate all of our tracker rings. He's going to call when he has a location for Sanchez."

Tristan's eyes flared. "Is her name really Maria? Because everyone just calls her Sanchez, so I didn't know what her first name was."

"Her name is really Maria." Kane had figured they all knew, but maybe she'd never told them.

Crew said, "Rio is on his way. He wants an ID on the guys who knocked over the bus, but he's at least an hour out."

"Right." Kane didn't plan on being here that long. Not when they were going to have a location soon and needed to get out there and get her back.

Kane swung his legs over the side of the bed.

"Someone is going to check you out before you leave." Crew eyed him. "You're not back on the hotshot team until you're cleared by a doctor, so don't take off before you get signed out by the doc. That's what Tucker told me to tell *all* of you. Almost like you guys have a tendency of not sticking around long enough to get checked out."

Kane said nothing.

"Once that happens, Tris and I will go with you to get her back."

Kane glanced between them. "Sure?"

"We know what we're doing, bro," Tristan said. "We're good to go, and we want these guys taken down as much as anyone. We're in this for the long haul. Something you should know by now."

Crew just stood there, as if what Tristan was

saying wasn't surprising. Maybe they'd talked about it while Kane was out.

He felt like he'd been hit by a truck—or a bus. Saxon was getting stitches. Neither of them was in any shape to go alone. "Help would be good."

But only because Hammer wasn't here. That guy was worth four guys put together, even guys like Kane. It was why he'd been their Delta Force team leader.

"It's settled, then." Tristan nodded.

"I want her location. Tell Tucker to hurry up."

Crew nodded and stepped out of the bay.

Kane turned to Tristan. "How is Logan?"

"The doctor keeps using terms like *chronic traumatic encephalopathy*, and Jamie is getting all teary-eyed." Tristan cleared his throat. "Apparently it's been bad for a few weeks, but he didn't tell anyone."

The guy talked a good game, but Tristan was probably just as nervous as Jamie, considering his sister was upset and the man she loved had a medical problem.

"Too many traumatic brain injuries. I've seen it before, and if it's this bad, he's probably not going to be fighting fire anymore." Kane winced. "Is Bryce here?"

Tristan frowned. "You know his family?"

"I'm from Last Chance County, but it's been a long time." Kane wasn't going to explain his own family tie to the Eastside Firehouse.

"Good to know." Tristan nodded. "Bryce and Penny, and Andi and Jude, are on their way. Their mom stayed with their dad."

That was likely what was making everyone nervous. Logan's father had a TBI that severely hampered his ability to have a normal life—but it didn't steal his enjoyment of fishing. With a nurse and plenty of family around to care for him, the Crawford siblings' father had a peaceful life. At least, he did now that their family wasn't the target of a dangerous cartel.

Still, with history seeming to repeat itself in Logan, they were probably all on edge.

"Thanks for the update." He held out his hand. "I appreciate it."

Tristan shook hands with Kane. "No problem. I'm just glad I can help. Better than feeling useless here." He stepped away from the end of the bed. "I'm gonna go see if Crew has a location for Sanchez."

Kane said, "Thanks."

He was all fine to stay put and let a doctor check him out, but after he took care of some pressing business. Which meant finding a restroom down the hall.

He was washing his hands when the door opened and a man stepped in.

Kane twisted around, the faucet still running, not exactly registering a threat, but close. He wasn't going to let his guard down with his back to the room.

Kane stared at the guy, and the pieces clicked into place. "I know who you are."

He'd only ever seen this man in a picture. Never in person. The older man nodded, lines permanently etched into the skin around his eyes and on his forehead, gray hair on the sides of his head, and a beard covering the lower half of his face. He looked too thin, almost sick. Definitely malnourished.

He said, "That makes this easier."

Kane shut off the water. "Doctor Cortez?"

"Rodrigo."

"Kane Foster."

"You're the one." The older man studied him. "Good."

"You know who I am?"

"I know you'll do everything you can to protect her. Is that right?"

Kane nodded. "That's right."

"You and your friends."

"Because I asked them to help me keep her safe."

Rodrigo was still for a moment, then nodded. "You have a way to find her?"

"We're working on it." Kane had a feeling this conversation was going to be over just as fast as it started, so he moved closer to the other man and grabbed a paper towel. Wiped his hands dry, using the movement to tug off his tracker ring. "Anything you can share that might help me do that?"

"It's too risky, me even being here, but they're all distracted with her. I need your assurance that she will get through this. Otherwise I can't do what I need to."

Kane didn't like the sound of this. "Maria wants to see you. She's been looking for you since you were taken from her."

"She's made a life for herself. Once she's free of these people, she'll be able to be happy."

"That won't happen without you."

Rodrigo looked aside at the bathroom stalls. "We both know what's at stake here. If I allow them to capture me again, this will never end. I'll die a captive."

"I have a friend in the FBI. He can help you—"

"You trust them?" Rodrigo laughed, the sound hollow. "One day they'll betray you. I've learned not to be surprised."

"This agent is one of the good ones. One of *us*." Rio was married to a smokejumper. He'd more than proven himself. "Please, come in. Stay somewhere you can be safe, where Maria can spend time with you after I get her back. She wants to see you."

Rodrigo was already shaking his head before Kane even finished. "Find her. That's your job—to keep her safe. My job is to finish this."

"I'm going to, but—"

"Good." The older man nodded, turning for the door. "I'm going to hold you to your promise. I expect you to protect her."

Kane followed him to the door, grabbing the wood above Rodrigo's head. He could see he'd thrown the man off guard, and Kane used the distraction to slip his tracker ring into the man's jacket pocket. "I can do that better if she and I know you're safe."

"What happens to me doesn't matter. Only that they are stopped, no matter what they try in order to get me to give up. Give in." Rodrigo lifted his chin. "Not even Maria's life will sway me. That's why it's up to *you*."

The door clicked shut and he was gone.

Kane whipped it open and stepped out into the hallway, looking both ways. "What does that mean?"

But Maria's father was gone.

Not even her life would sway her father to do anything but "finish" this? It sounded like he was determined, but also that he didn't care enough about his daughter to put her well-being above... thousands of lives? The destruction of the US economy? Those were high stakes, and maybe Kane didn't want to have to face a choice like that.

A choice between the country and the woman he loved.

All he knew was that he needed to find her before she was killed. Then they could worry about saving the world.

Together.

NINE

AT THE END OF THE EMPTY HALLWAY, she found a door. Maria didn't look back. She would see the man lying on the floor with pliers sticking out of his . . . *Don't think about that.*

She tucked her right hand against her body, holding her arm, and stepped into a sort of mud room. A heavy coat hung on a hook, so she slipped her arms into it, ignoring the pain. Breathing through gritted teeth.

Trying not to pass out.

They would realize soon enough that she'd escaped. Only God knew if she'd manage to get out the door and away from here to a place where she was safe.

Help me. Don't help me. Either way, I'm not staying here.

She used her off hand for the handle, and a rush of cool air from outside brushed her hair back from her face. Even that hurt. But she wasn't going to think about it.

She hadn't said anything.

He'd tried what he'd tried. When she'd grown exhausted, or so he'd thought—though, she'd only been slightly pretending, most of her reactions truthful—eventually he'd decided to give her a break. He'd told her he would come back later for round two.

Cue, escape.

Maria stumbled off the back step and headed for the trees, not the outbuilding. *Run.* It didn't matter how far she had to go or how long she would have to run. She would run all the way back to base camp if it came to it.

Hopefully it wouldn't.

Trees surrounded this homestead on all sides she could see. There had to be a fire road or some other kind of access, given they'd driven in. She remembered that much through her haze of semiconsciousness from the ride over after the bus crash.

Finding the road was the worst idea.

But then, if Kane was coming... so was leaving the house.

She ran anyway, until she stumbled and had to slow. Maria leaned against a tree and looked down at her mangled, broken fingers. The indent where the tracker ring should be.

He'd been interested in it and had cut it off her. Probably why he'd opted to give her a break—so he could show it to the others.

"Go." *Don't think.* If she stopped long enough for her thoughts to catch up, she would be lying in a ball in the dirt, crying.

Not a lifesaving tactic, even if sometimes it was necessary.

Later.

Shouts erupted behind her, back at the cabin.

Maria pushed off the tree and kept going, thinking about her stride. Her breaths. The angle of her hips and how her foot snapped forward again after she kicked it back. The kind of control that got a person through the stall to the end of a marathon.

Through the point where they felt as if they couldn't continue.

She hugged the coat against herself and just ran. "Don't stop." She needed the encouragement, even if it was only from herself.

In her mind, she imagined Kane beside her, urging her on the way he did in training. The way they all did. Cheering each other on with encouragements until things got dire and the encouragement became an order from a superior.

Don't quit.

You quit and people die. Are you gonna let that happen?

They'd been military trained. She'd been CIA trained. It was always life or death for them, and that was what it felt like for people who were about to lose everything because of a wildfire.

Maria stumbled and her elbow hit the ground first. Blinding white-hot pain sprang from her fingers up her arm. She pushed off with her other hand and stood, glancing over her shoulder.

Too far back to see her pursuers, but they were there.

Chasing her.

She had no clue what this terrain was like, but some of those militia guys had dogs. Elias wouldn't quit until he had her in his grasp again.

She couldn't hide and wait it out, even if the sky wouldn't darken for a few hours yet. It was far better to risk the dangers of the backcountry and keep going.

Don't stop.

This family doesn't quit.

A twig snapped to her left.

Maria spotted a black mass between the trees but wasn't going to slow down enough to meet that creature. She angled to the right, away from it. *Ignore me. Everything's fine.* She kept running.

Her head swam.

She sucked in some cleansing breaths.

A river would be nice. Except it would probably be ice-cold snow runoff. Even this time of year the water would be freezing. It would feel good, and it would numb her hand. But before long, it would kill her.

No rivers.

She stumbled to the side, and her shoulder glanced off a tree. She managed to choke back the cry that wanted to escape her lips and grabbed the next trunk with her free hand. Branches covered with pine needles scratched at her face. She wove between them, praying she disappeared into the darkness of the close-growing vegetation.

At least another half a mile she picked her way slowly in erratic directions.

The landscape started to slope down, hopefully bringing her to a valley. One with a busy highway or an airport. She would even settle for train tracks. Not that she could jump on a moving freight car right now.

Dirt beneath her boot moved with her, and she

surfed for a second. Maria held her arms tight to her front, resisting the urge to windmill them and keep her balance.

Her knee hit the dirt, and she waited a second, then pushed back up. Almost didn't make it. She was losing strength. Losing the wherewithal to keep going.

Run.

Or hide.

Like in that opening, the one that looked like a lifeline. Not like a bear cave. *God, I don't want to get mauled. Or captured.*

She needed rescue, but that would take a miracle.

Maria ducked her head. The cave was only an overhang with heavy growth on both sides. She sank to the ground, breathing hard, pain reverberating in every inch of her body. She turned, knowing she was going to hit the ground. Her shoulder landed in the dirt.

All her strength seemed to seep into the dirt beneath her feet.

Still, she could hear Kane yelling in her ear.

Maria gritted her teeth. "I can't do it."

She didn't have any more strength. This was it, the place where they'd find her. The spot where she would either die or be captured again for more questioning.

She shifted enough she could hold her arms in front of her, trying to lessen the pain at least a little. But it didn't. It never had. Not since she'd seen her mother die and her father taken from her.

She lay there, breathing hard. Her pulse throbbing in her temples.

Tears slid from her eyes, but crying just made her hurt more. She didn't want that. She didn't want to shed tears for that man. She shouldn't cry for her father. Not after he had escaped his captors and hadn't come looking for her.

She'd spent years looking for him. Training. Working missions. Going to the farthest, darkest corners of the world. Constantly trying to convince people he wasn't evil. That he hadn't turned on this country. He was a victim.

Maria had spent her life trying to rescue her father.

Now, when he was free, he hadn't come for her. He'd left her to fend for herself. Probably told those men that she knew the code, making her a target when he'd saved himself.

She looked down at her hands, both the broken one and the other. At least two of her fingers were bent in ways they shouldn't be. Blood coated her palms and fingers, dry now. The blood of the guy who'd been guarding the door, who would've killed her after those others had tortured her—and nearly did before she escaped, leaving him not breathing.

Life or death.

That was the life her father had given her. Even if not by his own choice, it was by his design that he'd been gone so long, considering he had the power to escape them now and he'd done it. He'd been on the run for weeks now and hadn't found her. Never once even called. He'd just sent her that nothing note and put her in danger. Maybe he didn't even care.

This was who she had been forced to become. The kind of woman now lying in the dirt, covered in blood, waiting for a miracle that wasn't going to come.

All of it for a man who didn't care.

It was after midnight when they stopped their ATVs outside a cabin—a remote homestead that had taken them far too long to reach.

Kane shut off his engine and swung his leg over, going first toward the front door. Gun out. Ready for whatever happened next.

"Itching for a fight."

Saxon had a point.

"Fine." He would slow down, ease up, and let them help him. Do this as a team.

Tristan said, "Did that make sense to anyone?"

Crew came up beside Tristan, and thankfully no one came out the front door or started shooting at them from any direction. It gave Kane a second to say, "What?"

Crew said, "You guys talk in shorthand."

"It's annoying." Tristan walked to the right. "I'll go around back."

"I'll go with him." Saxon jogged after Jamie's brother.

"I guess we have the front." Crew crossed the grass toward Kane. "You think his arm is really okay?"

Kane scanned the area. "Three stitches? He's fine." Tire grooves in the dirt. Trees too close together and too close to the house, which was the worst way it could be if a wildfire came through this area. "They were here."

"You think they're gone?"

"This is where her ring is." Kane kicked the front door because he needed to let out some of this tension, plus he could keep two hands on his gun and get the door open. Thankfully, it wasn't wired up to blow, because no one needed that.

Arctic entry, plenty of boots and coats. Skis stacked in the corner, and a snowboard hanging on the wall above his head. A place to don cold-weather gear and then leave the dirt and snow outside before you went into the house.

Inside smelled stuffy and wasn't all that warm. Someone had eaten but not cleaned up. The trash overflowed with beer cans and pizza boxes. Bare wood floors. Wainscoting on the walls. A couple of seventies-era paintings of mountains and bears on the walls, and one of those mechanical fish that sang—until you got sick of it.

"Living room is clear."

Saxon met him in the hall and tipped his head toward a door beside where he stood.

Kane lifted his chin. "Blood on the floor."

It disappeared under the door.

Saxon kicked the door open and went in first. A dead man lay slumped in the corner of the room.

"They dragged him in here to hide him." Saxon stepped back.

"This is where her ring pinged." Kane looked around. "This location. Maybe Maria did."

"You think she killed that guy?"

Kane scanned what he could see of the guy propped up in the corner. Blood on his neck and shirt, where it had trailed down from a wound on his head. "Looks like it was quick."

Saxon glanced over. "You know she would only kill in self-defense. Not sure she would bother hiding a body though."

"Where is she? And where are the rest of them?"

Crew wandered down the hall. "It looks like they cleared out in a hurry. Maybe they realized what the tracker ring was, and they took her and fled somewhere else."

"I like the idea of them being on the run," Kane admitted. "But not the idea we'll have no idea where to find her."

"Speaking of," Crew said. "Where's Tris?"

Saxon turned and headed for the back door and another artic entry–mudroom type of door. This area would get cold in the long winters, and whoever lived in this house preferred to stay indoors and only venture out when they were fully prepared with gear.

Kane stopped between the back doors.

"What is it?" Crew asked over his shoulder.

"That." He motioned to what he'd spotted, a smear of blood on the wall. "She was here."

"You know she was here, but you don't know that blood has anything to do with her."

"It's barely dry." Kane stepped outside and found Saxon talking to Tristan, over by the trees.

As he approached, they broke off their conversation.

"What is it?" Kane asked.

Tristan said, "I think she ran for it."

Saxon rolled his shoulders. "Alaska is a pretty big state for 'think,' because that idea of yours has us walking all over this landscape looking for her. That's like trying to find a pine needle in a stack of needles that has a grizzly bear hiding in it."

"Or a pack of militia guys. We have no idea where to start." Kane looked at Crew, then Tristan. Both of them knew all about the militia because they'd both gone undercover, trying to dig out the truth. They'd made strides and found victories in their own ways. On their terms.

Now it was his turn.

He looked back at the door to the cabin. Then he wandered to the woods, scanning the ground and the trees. Branches. Ruts in the dirt that could be footprints.

"She's your woman," Tristan said from behind him. "You think she made a run for it?"

He nearly said *She's not my woman* but didn't.

It was on the tip of his tongue to say, but it didn't matter what he claimed aloud. They all knew what he hadn't admitted to anyone. The rest of the people who lived at the Midnight Sun base camp were smart enough to see how he felt about her. How he figured she felt about him—not that they'd verbalized it. She was better at keeping her intentions in check.

"Let's look around." Kane headed into the woods and right away spotted blood on a tree. "She came this way."

They followed him. He knew because he could hear them behind him. No one said anything while he picked his way between trees and over fallen logs. Making good time through the woods, holding a steady pace. Looking for any signs of Maria.

Thinking about what, for Tristan, had been a throwaway comment, no doubt. For Kane, it represented everything he wanted.

Your woman.

It might not be so politically correct these days, but he had to admit, sometimes he did want to throw her over his shoulder and carry her off. Convince her to marry him.

Whoa.

Hold up. Neither of them had said *marriage*,

and he certainly hadn't thought it. But that would be the natural end of this, wouldn't it? That he'd ask her to be in his life forever, permanently, in a way that meant he could honor her for the rest of their days. Cherish her. Learn more about her every day and how to love her the best way he could.

Because a woman who gave everything to rescue someone was the kind of woman he wanted in his life. She was the kind of mother he wanted his children to have, rather than the parents he'd had. They'd done their best, but when life had become tough, they'd retreated. They'd certainly never stuck it out no matter what, the way she did.

Still, first they had to take down Elias Redding and secure that canister. Stop the plot. Give or take whatever Rodrigo was planning to do.

They were so close to ending this he could almost taste it. Once he found Maria, maybe he would tell her how he felt but ask her to hang on with him. To stick it out, and after this was done, they'd figure out where they were going next.

Even if they'd never talked about the future, always focusing on what was right in front of them. Aware of the stakes because their business was life or death for innocent people, and that always came first.

At the expense of their lives sometimes.

Because that was the truth, wasn't it? They might save the day, but it might also cost them a life together. It was a price they were willing to pay, and at the same time, it was expected that they'd offer it up.

"Over here." Saxon stood at the edge of a decline.

Not sharp, the terrain angled down, and Kane spotted an animal trail that snaked its way between the trees.

Blood was smeared on one of the branches. Just a smudge.

"She ran, and they left?" he said.

Behind him, Saxon said, "Looks that way. They probably figured she wouldn't survive. Or it would take too long to find her out here."

Kane stumbled to the entrance of a little overhang that shielded the inside from the elements. But it wouldn't protect a person from cold wind. It wasn't deep enough for an animal to call home.

She was curled up in the dirt, asleep or unconscious.

He landed on his knees and touched her cheek. "Maria." She was so cold, even in the jacket. But under his fingers, her pulse beat steady.

Behind him, Saxon hissed. "Looks like someone took a hammer to her fingers."

Kane didn't look, but he assessed her for other injuries and didn't find any wounds. "We need to get her out of here."

He stuck his gun in the back of his belt and slid his arms under her and lifted her, leaving the cave, even though he'd rather have curled up with her. Roaring fire. Blankets. Protecting her from everything and everyone that wanted to harm her.

A ring on her finger.

Another on his.

Together. Always.

"Let's go."

TEN

HE'S THE ONE WHO BROKE YOUR fingers? This Chinese guy?"

Maria wanted to squirm under the intensity of Hammer's stare. The bearded Delta Force team leader sat in a chair beside the hospital bed, his hands clasped in front of him and his elbows on his knees.

"Sanchez."

She nodded. "Yes. Which means I'm out of the hotshots for the rest of the season, and Tucker is going to have to get others in to fill in for us." Her. Logan. "I don't like it."

"Is that what you're most worried about?"

Of course not. "I'm just . . . listing it among my grievances."

She'd woken up half an hour ago, no one else in

here but Hammer. Because Kane knew—he *knew* she didn't want to wake up in the hospital alone. They all knew she didn't want a crowd either. She didn't want a doctor she didn't know.

So many things. Concessions they made for her.

Maybe she shouldn't lean on them so much, but they were her guys. She needed them.

"Thank you."

Hammer shook his head. "As if you have to say that." He sat back in his chair. "He's in the hall, you know. Probably wants to come in here and throw me out so he can sit with you and ask all the questions I'm asking. But we need to move on this intel." He reached down under the chair and lifted a laptop, which he set on the bed by her legs. "This has a database on it. Key players, people we know. Intel we've gathered and what we've been given access to by friends and associates. I want this Chinese guy ID'd."

Hot tears gathered in her eyes. She was *not* going to cry.

Kane had found her. He and Saxon, Crew and Tristan, had followed the GPS for her ring and found her in the woods. They'd made it so she wasn't alone when she woke up.

"Elias thinks he's going to get the code," she

said. "He thinks his plan will come to pass because he isn't going to give up."

Hammer said, "We're all fighting this one. Even your father, from what you said. He's doing what he has to do. It might not be what he wants to do, but he knows it's best for everyone."

She'd told him that her father was out there, and about the note. Even if she didn't consider that him "contacting" her. Regardless of if it was his handwriting, it wasn't anything close to closure.

She'd told Hammer everything, because that's how it was between them. He, Saxon, and Kane, and by extension Mack as well, were the best kind of men. She'd struck gold when they'd rescued her. Careening into her life with war paint on their faces, carrying guns and packs and all kinds of gear. Talking about exfils and rendezvous and eating MREs.

She'd discovered all of a sudden that she wasn't alone.

And they hadn't stopped there. They'd jumped on board with her life after they'd been declared dead. Not even one single thought of going back home and digging up proof they hadn't gone to the dark side. No, they'd decided together that going with her and finding her dad and, by extension, Elias Redding, was what would set everything to rights.

Just like that.

As if it was that easy to change your whole life. Or put it on hold. All to do the right thing, save the world. Clear their names. Save her and her father.

In one swoop, they'd set everything back the way it should be.

"I knew you guys would come to find me."

Hammer said, "I did what I could to help, but I was deployed. Not sure I'm gonna jump again with the team soon though. You took years off my life."

"Is Mack okay?"

Hammer's expression shuttered. "The kid knows how to take a beating and bounce back. Even if it's a bus doing the hitting."

"You got him out. That's what you do." She needed him to know. "You're a rescuer."

"Turns out I'm not." He gave her a small smile. "I just do what God put it in me to do."

"God?" He'd never talked about faith before. Did he believe now?

"Go figure. Being around all these Christians the last two years? It's rubbing off. Logan told me that God made me who I am."

"The guy who rescues people."

Hammer said, "I wanted to be there to rescue your father."

"Me too."

"Maybe he'll show up."

Whatever that meant. "Let's worry more about Elias and this canister."

"He thinks you have the code. That means he could come back," Hammer said. "He could try to snatch you again and get you to talk." He motioned to her hand.

The doctor had done an X-ray and immobilized her hand. Maria didn't like it, but considering the million ways this could have gone worse, she didn't have much to complain about. She could write and shoot with her off hand.

Though, right now, maybe that was just the pain killers talking.

"If he does come back," she said, "maybe we could be ready for him." She liked the sound of that. Turning the tables. Getting revenge.

"You want to trap him, take him down?"

"After what he did to you guys, I want to do a lot more than that." She cleared her throat. Maybe just after being captured and tortured herself. Not like what some people had to go through. But enough she wanted to kill Elias more than ever now.

He studied her expression. "What's this now?"

She pretended she didn't know what he was talking about. Who wanted to admit they had vengeance on their mind? "What are you talking about?"

"You aren't telling me something."

Her stomach clenched. "It doesn't matter."

He stood, moving to the side of the bed. "I think it does."

Of course he would see it.

She gritted her teeth. Shook her head.

"I get that you don't feel good right now. You might need a minute. But you'd only be hiding." He leaned down. "Talk."

"He was my . . . asset."

Hammer didn't move. "You knew him before he captured you?"

She nodded. "I'd learned he was part of the group holding my father, so I figured that he'd know where to find my dad." She had to take a breath before she could continue. "So I worked him like an asset. Got him to trust me, and he started to show me intel about the group."

"You didn't know who he was?"

She shook her head. "I had no idea he wasn't a

contractor. That he was Delta Force and part of your team. I never saw you guys with him. When I met him, he was usually alone."

"What happened?"

"We only met a couple of times. Then someone turned me over to some Russians in Syria. They had a deal going with the locals. While I was there, thinking somehow I'd made a misstep and been found out, he showed up. That's when I knew it was him who'd betrayed me."

Hammer said, "But Langley knew you'd been snatched and sent us to find you."

"Elias would've known he couldn't show up there with your team. When I realized later that he was part of it, I figured he probably betrayed you because he'd have been found out. Or it was a convenient time to put the plan into place. I don't know." Her breath hitched. "Maybe he double-crossed the three of you *because* of me. After all, his people and the ones holding me would've realized he was playing both sides. They probably would've thought he was a US double agent, and they'd have killed him."

Hammer said, "He probably plans to claim that if he's caught, even now. Probably plans to drag my team through the mud and make us look like the traitors so he goes free and we get life in a military prison."

"I'm not going to let that happen. I was there. I know the truth." She wanted to grab his hand but had to remember to do that with her left. The one with the IV. She held on like she was holding on for dear life. And maybe that's what she'd been doing with them for two years. "He can't win. He'll destroy too many lives."

"So then ID the guy who hurt you." Hammer held her gaze with a steady one. "And let me finish this. Before anyone else is destroyed."

Maria sniffed back tears. She couldn't even voice what she'd been thinking about her father and the fact he hadn't come to find her. She might be able to tell Kane though. In fact, she needed him in here so she could see for herself that he was all right.

She couldn't believe that after those guys had crashed the bus and taken her, he'd bounced back from the hospital to come all the way up to that homestead and find her.

Wading in to save her yet again.

Kane.

"Do me a favor?" Hammer said. "Think about what they all say about Jesus and God's grace. It's worth listening to."

She stared at him, unsure this was even the same man who'd led a team into Syria to rescue her. "Really?"

He nodded. "Really."

"Okay. I'll listen."

"You know, he did us a favor that day."

Maria frowned. "What do you mean?"

"Elias. He cost us a teammate—him. But he gave us you." He leaned down and kissed her forehead. "I'll take that trade any day."

"This was really your highest priority for today?"

Kane gripped the wheel of Saxon's 4Runner, which he'd borrowed specifically to take Sanchez from the hospital back to the base so she could rest in her own bed and they'd all be nearby to take care of her. "Can't think of anything I'd rather be doing."

"Baloney sandwiches."

He laughed. "I'm not lying."

"Spill."

At least she was in good spirits. That counted for something, right? She might have some bouts of grief or sadness when she was alone, or frustration when she had a hard time getting changed or one of the girls had to help her shower for a while.

Right now, she was smiling in the passenger seat, the splinted, bandaged hand on her lap.

"Talk, Kane."

"Okay." He reached over and squeezed her knee. She didn't need to beg, and neither of them needed to joke about fun ways to torture information out of each other.

If that happened *never,* it would be too soon.

"Tucker ordered me and Saxon to take the smokejumpers' qualifier test."

"Ordered?"

Kane pulled onto the highway out of Copper Mountain and headed toward the base camp. A crack of lightning splintered the sky, lighting up the heavy clouds.

"Whoa." She shifted in her seat.

Rain started to patter against the windshield. "It's coming down."

"We'll have more fires tomorrow."

"Right," Kane said. "Logan is out. Hammer can cover one slot, but we need alternates if anything else happens like Orion reinjuring himself. Now that you're off the hotshots, he's panicking. He wants Mitch, Grizz, Raine, and Mack to join a group from the Bureau of Land Management, get absorbed into their crew, and he wants to strengthen numbers and get the smokejumpers on a good footing for the remainder of the season."

"He *ordered* you?"

"It was Hammer's idea." Kane glanced over, but with the lightning flashing and the rain coming down in sheets, he needed to keep his focus on the road. A peel of thunder rumbled the car. "Don't be mad."

"Why would I be mad? This is what you trained for. You've jumped out of how many planes with Delta Force?"

"We weren't paratroopers, but we know how to jump."

"There you go. It makes sense."

Kane wasn't so sure she was as okay with this as she was making out.

"One day after a bus crash where you're all tossed around, and you're jumping out of a plane. Makes perfect sense."

There it was. "You know what we did. The kind of men we are."

"It's beginning to dawn on me."

"As opposed to the one-woman save-the-world show?"

"You opted for the military. You chose that life."

Kane grinned. "I like my backup next to me when I'm being shot at, not on the other end of the phone—or at a safe house on the other side of the city."

"Made it easier to hide the fact I was looking for my father."

Kane tapped the brake. "My ring."

"What?"

"I dropped it in your dad's pocket."

"You saw my *father*?"

He nearly smacked his head on the steering wheel. "We got your location, and we rushed out to find you. I forgot to tell Jade I put my ring in your dad's pocket after he told me I'd better find you."

"You need to get a new one," she said. "Do not go out smokejumping into the middle of nowhere with no tracker ring. Promise me, Kane Foster."

She seemed to be more worried about him right now than she was about her father.

Given what she'd been through, he expected her emotions to be all over the place. But the fact was, if she didn't want to ask about her dad, she had a good reason.

Whatever it was, she cared more about his safety right now.

He reached over and took her good hand, lifted it, and planted a kiss on the back. "I promise I'll be safe. I'm not going to tell you not to worry about me, because I know you will. But I'll be okay. I'll have the whole team to watch out for me."

"While I'm sitting back in the cabin feeling sorry for myself, trying to open the peanut butter with one hand. Spending all day talking to Jubal because everyone else is busy saving the day."

He kissed her hand again.

"That isn't going to appease me. You aren't going to be out there with no way for anyone to find you. I'm not going to back down about this. You aren't going to break my resolve." She started to laugh, but it quickly dissolved into great big body-racking sobs that made his heart feel like it was going to burst out of his chest.

Kane hit the brakes and steered to the side of the road. He threw the car into Park and unbuckled both of their seatbelts, then dragged her over the center console onto his lap.

"You can't fix everything."

"I can try." He tugged her close, his arms around her, being careful of her injured hand.

If she put up a fight, it was only on principle

and it didn't last long. He wasn't going to turn this into a battle, even though that was the way she was wired.

"Let go," he said. She'd been holding on to all of it for so long she probably didn't even know how. "Let it go."

She sobbed, swiping her face with her good hand. "I don't need to do anything. I'm not going to com-plain." A sob interrupted her. "I'm not going to wail about how t-terrible it is. This is what I do. I s-survive this stuff."

"I know."

"I got myself out."

"I know."

"I killed that guy to get away because he gave me no choice."

"I know." He held on to her, rubbing a hand up and down her back. "You got out, and you hid long enough for me to find you."

"I would've made it on my own."

"But you didn't have to." Kane felt tears burn in his eyes. "You know I wouldn't have left you out there alone."

"I know." She gripped a handful of his shirt and held on. "I knew you'd be there. All of you. That the Trouble Boys wouldn't let me down."

Her words settled in him with a note of disquiet.

She still saw the Trouble Boys as a team, drawing a line of distinction between her and *them* instead of considering her and *him*.

"The rest of the team isn't here." His arm settled around her waist, his hand on her hip. With the other, he touched her cheek. Swiped away a tear. "Just me. And you."

"Kane." She whispered his name.

"No matter what."

"I know that."

"Do you?" He needed an answer. She knew what he was asking. "I feel like I'm putting it all on the line, waiting for you to give a signal. A green light. I know it's probably better to wait until the mission is over and we get our lives back. But I nearly lost you today."

He'd seen Elias in that bus, dragging her away.

Kane had flashed back in his mind to being a captive of Elias and his men. Just for sport. Not for any other reason except that he *could*. Those men had entertained themselves by cutting and burning his back, shredding Kane down bit by bit while he'd plotted and planned how to escape.

But he hadn't rescued himself. Not the way Maria had.

His team had come for him.

"I nearly lost you," he said again.

Her breath caught in her throat. "You didn't. I'm right here." She leaned in, just a little. "With you."

Kane's hand tightened on her hip.

He waited.

She eased forward, bracing against his chest. Doing what she needed to do to keep her other hand from getting bumped. Maria leaned in while the rain pounded on the car and lightning lit the interior. He saw the light in her eyes a second before she touched her lips to his.

Kane tilted his head to the side and let her set the pace, even though he wanted nothing more than to sweep them both away. Tighten his hold on her, kiss her until she understood precisely what he'd been feeling for two years. Since the day he'd found her in that cell in Syria. Through the days he'd been a captive until they found him. And every day since then.

Followed by every day for the rest of his life. Unless they ended the misery he was in—with her, but unable to have her the way he thought God might intend. Around her, but never able to tell her how he really felt. Partners. Friends.

So much more, just out of reach.

All this sweetness and he'd never even known. He soaked it in now like a starving man. He drank her in, trying to fill himself up, knowing it would never be enough.

She stilled and eased back a little. "Well . . ." She chuckled.

He liked the sound of it.

"My hand hurts, but you're a pretty good distraction."

Kane said, "Happy I could help."

"Did you really drag me onto your lap?"

"I needed to make a point."

"Hmm." She shifted in his lap. Probably trying to figure out how to get back over to her side. "It was a good point."

"I think you might've made one of your own."

"You can remember it when you're smokejumping, and then you'll be safe and come back to base when it's done."

"Yes, ma'am."

She eased her way back to her side with an audible sigh. "What am I going to do with you?"

"I can think of a few things."

"Do they involve driving me back to base camp so I can take more meds and sleep for days?"

"Um . . . definitely." Kane grinned, pulling back onto the highway.

It might be pouring rain right now, but tomorrow the sun would come up, and things would be different.

They hadn't finished this. It wasn't over.

But whatever happened, they had taken another step to being what he needed them to be.

Together.

ELEVEN

YOU'RE SERIOUS? HE KISSED YOU!" JoJo practically bounced up and down on the end of Maria's bed. "That's great!"

"I don't know if that's the word I'd use." Monumental. Earth-shattering, maybe? "I need to get dressed, and you need to go train." She used her good hand to toss the sweater at JoJo.

"Later, I want *all* the details."

Maria nodded. JoJo helped her thread her hand through the sleeve and buttoned it for her. "Help me tie my shoes?"

"Of course, girl. No one is gonna leave you hanging." JoJo sat cross-legged in front of her and laced up her sneakers. "I know you're the lone wolf and all . . ."

"You know that correlating people and wolves doesn't always work," Maria pointed out.

"Except when it does. Like you, Ms. Lone Wolf. But you have a pack, in case you didn't notice."

Maria would've said the Trouble Boys were family, but JoJo was talking about all the hotshots and smokejumpers. "I know. Dani, Grizz, Crew, Tristan, and Jamie are gonna meet me in the mess hall so we can figure out what we know. What we need to find out."

"And you'll tell Dani or Jamie if you need help with anything... personal? It won't be easy trying to do it one-handed."

"I'll ask for help." As much as it might irk her to do that.

"Speaking of..."

Maria frowned. "What now?"

JoJo chuckled. "I guess you're feeling pretty off-kilter since that man kissed all the reason out of your brain last night."

"You make it sound salacious. It was sweet." In a very *Kane* kind of way.

"Mmm. Mr. Tall, Dark, and Brooding has hidden depths we love in all honorable alpha males. It's good to know he's not messing around."

He definitely hadn't been messing around. "Just tell me what you were gonna say."

She didn't want to get distracted with thoughts about Kane. That happened plenty, including when she was supposed to have been trying to sleep last night. The man had driven her back to base camp, held her hand while he walked her to the cabin, and kissed her under the eave. Short and sweet, but it had reminded her of that drag-me-across-the-console, lay-one-on-me-like-you-mean-it make-out session in the car. Talk about hot and bothered.

She was going to blame it on the two broken fingers.

Maybe she had a fever.

JoJo said, "Jade told me Crispin is back from one of his super-secret missions. He might want to help out if y'all are going to save the world. I guess it's still his thing now, like it was in Montana." She skimmed her gaze over Maria's hair. "Want a braid?"

"Do it fast." Maria turned around, one knee bent on the bed.

"Shame we don't have time for two full Viking war braids, because you'd look like one of those tough Hispanic MMA fighters. But we'll make do with the time we have." JoJo fixed her hair, then grabbed her things and headed out to join the smokejumpers.

Maria called out "Thanks!" a second before the front door slammed, shaking the cabin.

She got her laptop in her backpack all zipped up and swung it over her good shoulder. Outside, the sky had cleared, but she could see the haze of smoke in the sky. Lightning from last night's storm had caused a few new wildfires to spring up, but the Bureau of Land Management had crews out working those. Their hotshots would join them this morning.

The smokejumpers were all in front of the hangar, across the runway.

She wasn't going to look for Kane. He needed to do his job without worrying about her, and she had things to do herself.

He had been right that it was better to wait until this situation was over, but knowing he'd been harboring the same feelings for her that she had for him gave her enough peace to keep moving forward.

Not just that, but she'd broken down and gotten all emotional about what had happened, bleeding it off like pressure-cooker steam. He hadn't freaked out and shut down or tried to fix it. He'd held her. Been there for her with that steady strength.

That was why she'd kissed him.

Because he'd been there for her since they met, sticking with her through it every day. On mission with her. For the first time, she'd felt like part of a team, even if the Trouble Boys were their own group and she was the one they were protecting.

The shift last night had been seismic in proportions. Maybe it had started with Hammer's words, which she was going to hold close and cherish. Then Kane had drawn a dividing line between the two of them and Hammer and Saxon.

Because what she and Kane had was different from what she had with any of the others. Now they both knew it. They'd discovered *why* when she'd touched her lips to his and the fire nearly consumed them both.

"Great situational awareness."

She took a step and nearly fell down the porch steps, turned at the same time and spotted a dark-haired man on the chair by the door, an open Bible on his lap. "Crispin. You nearly scared me to death."

He set the Bible aside and stood. "Sorry. You were pretty deep in thought."

"I'm headed to the mess hall for a meeting. Are you in?" She figured he knew enough about what was going on that she didn't need to explain.

"Actually, I'm your bodyguard."

Maria frowned.

"He isn't paying me." Crispin lifted a hand, his expression soft, though the man could be tough—even scary—when he wanted to be. He had that edge to him that only disappeared when Jade was around. "And he didn't ask. I volunteered."

Fine. "Thanks."

They headed across the runway to the mess hall, where the others were already gathered. Maria handed Dani her laptop and looked around. "Where's Tristan?"

Dani shrugged. "Saw him talking to Raine between the hangar and this building. Neither of them looked happy."

Jamie said, "She's been asking questions about Tristan, like she's digging for information and trying to be sly about it."

"Information about what?"

"I have no idea, and I'm due back at the hospital soon. Logan has more tests this morning." Jamie dragged over Maria's laptop and started typing. "Did you find anything on her grandfather's hard drive?"

Maria shook her head. "I couldn't go through every document, but he seems clean. It was just a lot of invoices and shipping notices for barrels of gasoline. Though, I'm not sure why he'd need so much."

"Supplying communities up here with gas for generators. Plus, some planes use regular gas."

"Which fits with what we were thinking. That he's either innocent or he's removed enough he can deny all knowledge of their activities because we have *nothing*."

Grizz lowered his coffee mug. "Doesn't mean he's innocent. But I guess that's up to Rio to dig out. He's the one who questioned the guy and released him."

"But we don't think he's clean, right?" Dani glanced around. "I've been looking into Raine's family"—she winced—"which sounds bad, but it wasn't pointless, because I found out something interesting."

"Is it going to help us find Elias Redding and that canister?" Maria sat on the table, her feet on the bench seat.

Dani scrunched up her nose. "Unfortunately, it might." She paced a little, as if she needed to move to keep the tension in her from building too high. "Her father is Brian Howards."

Crew made a noise low in his throat. "Say that again."

Dani winced. "He was the leader of the militia

group that you ran into first. The group that Crew infiltrated." She glanced at Jamie, who looked a little shell-shocked. "But it doesn't seem like they had much of a relationship. He wasn't a good guy. In and out of jail for stretches. She lived with her mother and went to school in Anchorage."

"He was still her dad." Maria couldn't imagine finding out someone you knew had gone up against your father and considered him the enemy. Raine would have considered herself stained by her dad's actions, even if they weren't close.

Guilty by association.

"That's why she said she was hiding here." Like making amends—for who her father was. Maria could certainly understand that.

"We killed him," Jamie said quietly. "He came into the room that day when we were trying to escape. Logan, Tristan, and I were in the room. He was at the door."

Crew said, "I wasn't there."

"Tristan shot him."

Maria looked at the door. "Why did you say Raine wanted to talk to Tristan?"

Jamie stood abruptly, almost falling. "Maybe she knows he's the one who killed her dad."

Crew ran to the door and hauled it open right as a gunshot sounded from outside.

Kane spun around and started running, even with all the gear on—the flight suit and the helmet with the wire plate to keep his face from getting scratched up by trees. He tore the helmet off as he raced toward the sound of the gunshot.

People poured out of the mess hall.

Kane raised a hand. "Stay back!" He stopped at the corner of the hangar building and looked around.

Tristan had Raine pinned up against the outside wall of the hangar, a thunderous expression on his face. She stared up at him, boxed in, angry beyond all measure. But which one of them had tried to shoot the other?

"Tris!"

The guy didn't move.

As Kane closed in on them, he saw Tristan had hold of Raine's wrist. She held the gun, and with Tristan pinning her where she was, the gun was pointed up in the air.

"Give me the weapon." At this point, it didn't matter who had control of it. Kane reached over and put his hand around the gun. "Both of you let go."

"What's going on?" Tucker strode over, his expression pinched. "Who fired that weapon?"

Kane had control of it now. A revolver, and it was old. He pushed the cylinder to the side and tipped the rounds onto the ground.

Tristan let go of Raine and stepped back. "I did."

She flinched. Surprise flashed across her face.

"Is that what happened?" Tucker asked.

"I fired the weapon." Tristan turned to the commander. "It was my fault."

Kane watched Raine react to Tristan's words.

"Come with me." Tucker walked away, and Tristan went with him. Crew jogged after them.

Half the smokejumpers and everyone who'd been in the mess hall stood watching.

"Wanna tell me the truth?" Kane pinned Raine with a stare.

"It's just what Tristan said." She shrugged, not looking at him or anyone else. Suddenly finding the grass on the mountain behind the hangar extremely interesting.

"Right. You think I'm gonna believe that?"

Mitch strode over from the group by the mess hall door—a group that included Maria. But aside from a general assessing glance, Kane wasn't going to get distracted by her right now. This could be a serious situation.

Mitch said, "People on my team are people I trust. That means you tell me the truth."

Raine pushed off the side of the hangar where Tristan had pinned her.

"Is this your gun?" Kane asked. "Or your grandpa's?"

"Doesn't matter."

She really thought that? Kane wanted an answer as to what had just happened between Raine and Tristan. He hadn't seen them interact before, but maybe there had been something going on this entire summer.

"Tell us what that was." Kane had to bank on the relationship the hotshots had built. Otherwise, what else did they have? He didn't know much about this woman and her personal life, but he respected her. She was an amazing firefighter, someone who didn't give up.

The kind of woman who kept going through any situation.

Never quit.

She was cut from the same cloth as Maria.

"You can trust us, Raine." He studied her, praying she would open up.

Maria came over, close enough she held on to

his side with her good hand. Kane resisted the urge to put his arm around her. Everyone already knew the deal—he and Maria had simply been the last ones to get on board with what was going on. At least, he figured that was what'd happened.

Maria leaned against him. "Does this have to do with your father?"

Kane frowned. He needed to be caught up with what they were saying.

Before he could ask, Maria said, "He's the one who fired the shot that killed your dad, but that doesn't mean it was murder."

Raine's expression twisted with a mix of grief and anger. "He killed Brian."

"Tristan?" Kane looked over his shoulder and found Crispin. The other man nodded. "We know Tris. He isn't a murderer. He's Jamie's brother. If no one intervened, would you have killed him?"

Raine stared at the roof of the mess hall, determinedly not looking at any of them.

"Would you have ended his life?" Maria asked. "For the sake of a bad guy who wasn't even in your life all that much, right? I'm sorry, but it's true, isn't it?"

Raine said, "He was my father."

"I know what it's like to want something you don't have."

Kane shifted so he could put his arm around Maria.

She continued, "I know what it's like to want to have your father in your life but he can't be there, or he chooses not to be."

Kane said, "You can trust us. We understand more than you think."

His father had tried his best but had worked all the time so they'd have enough money. It had meant he did every scrap of overtime he could get his hands on for the paycheck. It was always about the paycheck. Gramps was the one who'd taught Kane how to be a man, until he died in that crash.

Raine said, "Yeah? You understand that Robert is dying? That he has cancer and there's nothing anyone can do? When he's gone, I won't have a single relative worth anything still alive. I'll be alone." Her voice broke on the last word, and she cleared her throat.

"I'm sorry." Maria shifted, hugging her injured hand to her front. "I know what that feels like. But you and I have talked about this place. About finding a family here with the team. Let us help you."

Kane figured Raine had been bottling it up for a while, keeping to herself, given she'd chosen to try and shoot Tristan instead of coming to someone with her concerns. Did she really think they were harboring a murderer? Raine couldn't believe Tristan had killed her father for any other reason than self-defense.

"We can't all have a team of guys watching out for us," Raine said. "Some of us are actually alone, not whatever it is you're pretending to be."

Maria flinched.

Kane said, "Raine, that was uncalled for. You know Maria's situation as well as anyone."

"I guess it's just me that can't do the super-secret stuff and get away with whatever I want." Raine looked away, effectively dismissing them.

Mitch strode over to their huddle. "Okay, smokejumpers, back to training. Hotshots, with me."

Kane turned and spotted Jade talking quietly with Crispin. The smokejumper team leader kissed him on the cheek and headed away from the group.

Maria touched Kane's arm.

He glanced at her. "Are you going to be okay?"

Maria said, "We'll figure it out."

Kane kissed her on the cheek. "Gotta go to work. Tucker just told us there's a flare-up happening about a hundred miles northwest of here.

Sounds like a nasty fire, and it's headed toward a small community."

"Be careful."

He jogged away, and Saxon caught up as he rounded the corner. Saxon said, "I knew she had it in her, but that was unexpected."

Kane said, "Raine?" He had to pray that Maria and the rest of them were safe. That nothing else happened while he was gone.

"Some people . . . you can see it in them."

"The potential for murder?"

Saxon shook his head. "Just a darkness. Unresolved feelings. Shadows. They've been abandoned too many times. They keep to themselves."

"So now every introvert is a murderer."

Saxon shoved his shoulder. "They'll both be fine."

"Only because I know those shadows. I was there. Maria with a gun? I have no problem. Someone like Raine? She needs a Bible study, not a weapon."

Saxon chuckled. "Guess we gotta go be smokejumpers."

Yeah, that was the problem, wasn't it? "She said she was fine with it. No problems. Come back to me, I'll see you later. Stay safe."

"And that's a bad thing?"

"She didn't have to be so . . . fine with it."

Saxon burst out laughing. "You want your woman to beg you to stay?"

"Shut up." He shoved his buddy in return.

They caught up with Jade at the plane.

"Ready to go, boss." Kane was happy to make this as quick as they could so he'd be back here watching out for Maria as soon as possible.

"Right. You know the drill," Jade said. "I've explained it."

Saxon said, "We've lived it."

Jade rolled her eyes. "Blah blah, you've both jumped more times than the rest of us put together. War zones. Insurgents. Etcetera. This is fire."

"We know how to fight a fire. We've been doing that for two seasons now," Kane pointed out.

"That's the only reason I'm okay with this." Jade glanced in the direction of the group they'd left behind. "I'm less okay with the rest of them working the whole terrorism thing while we're gone, but Crispin doesn't usually need my help with that stuff."

Kane frowned. "What do you mean?"

Jade shrugged. "The best way to resolve this is to call Rio, then have Sanchez contact Elias.

Tell him she'll give him the code if he leaves all the hotshots and smokejumpers and her father alone. She goes in because she insists he meet her in person, and they draw out Elias. Rio snaps the trap shut. Crispin and I figured it all out."

Kane turned back to the group so he could march over and tell Maria in no uncertain terms to *not* do that. At least, not while he wasn't there to make sure she was in no danger.

Or not *much* danger, anyway.

Saxon grabbed Kane's jumpsuit and dragged him back toward the plane. "Ready to deploy, boss."

"That's what I thought." Jade backed up and hopped on the plane, where everyone was already loaded and ready to go.

Lord . . .

He didn't even know what to pray for.

"She'll be fine. You think Crispin or Rio are going to let anything happen to her?"

Kane said, "I hate everything about this situation."

Saxon clapped a hand on Kane's shoulder. "Soon as we're back, you can pitch in."

Kane didn't want to, but he settled into a seat on the plane. They had to get through this jump to get qualified as smokejumpers so they could do their jobs. No one was going to leave the crew high and dry without enough people to fill the teams.

Orion looked over from the seat in front. "You good, Kane? You look kinda nervous."

"I'm not the one I'm worried about."

Through the window, he saw Maria out in front of the mess hall. She lifted her good hand and waved. He lifted his and pressed his palm to the window. He had to trust God, that He had Maria in His hands. There was no other option.

He'd stuck close, believing God had put him there beside her to make sure she was safe.

Now he had to trust God for real in a way he realized he didn't like.

Because he wouldn't be there.

TWELVE

MARIA HAD BEEN TUCKED INTO THE passenger side of Crew's truck. Crispin drove, Crew and Tristan in the back. She'd gone from having a three-man team of ex-Delta Force guys watching out for her to having three men of dubious background and an entire team of cops.

FBI. State police. The local sheriff.

All of them were going to be here for this.

"I know why you didn't tell me what we were doing before Kane left." In fact, she figured it was entirely by design that Jade was the smokejumper boss and in charge of their training today while Crispin—her partner in crime in all things except her job—told Maria what the plan was.

Crispin pulled into the parking lot of the Midnight Sun Saloon, full of cars since it was nearly lunch. The local crowd looking for a break mid-shift. Hopefully it wouldn't be too rowdy. Then again, the fewer people were in there, the higher the cop-to-civilian ratio would be. Something Elias would notice.

Crew said, "Dani just texted me. Elias is gonna be here in half an hour. He agreed to meet."

"Thanks." Crispin shut off the truck and turned to her.

"I'm fine. You don't need to say it."

"Your boyfriend needs to fight fires."

"I know that. I told him to go do it." She wanted to brush hair back from her face, but her right hand was no-go right now with all the bandages. Geez, it hurt just lifting her hand up. And leaving it in her lap. And when it was by her side. And when she moved.

"The others need to go do their jobs. That leaves you with us."

Tristan leaned forward from the backseat. "The poor man's Delta Force."

Crew chuckled. "I'm not telling JoJo you called us that. She'll tell Jamie, and then we'll be in trouble."

Maria said, "Seems like Tristan might already be in trouble, even if Raine and the other hotshots were moved to a BLM crew."

Tristan waved a hand. "Don't worry about it. Tucker banned me from the base camp, but I wanna be out here working anyway. We can't find this guy and the canister by sitting around in the mess hall."

"And Raine?" Maria needed to know what his intentions were. After all, it had looked like Raine tried to kill him since she knew now that he'd killed her father. Even given the circumstances, she had every right to be upset. But finding a gun and trying to shoot someone was entirely different.

"Don't worry about Raine." Tristan's jaw flexed. "I'll figure it out."

"Good thing Tucker didn't call the sheriff." Maria wasn't the kind to call cops, but Tucker was friends with the local lawman. A good guy by all accounts.

Which he needed to be if she was supposed to trust him with this operation.

Tristan said, "I explained the situation. Tucker is cool."

"We need to get in there." Crispin lifted his chin.

Maria spotted Rio across the parking lot, dressed in plain clothes. A lot like a local who worked in construction, wearing dark blue Dickies pants with cargo pockets, and a gray T-shirt with short sleeves showing off his tattoos. The ink had persuaded guys in jail he was one of them and not a Fed.

Crew had met Rio in prison and had become his confidential informant after Rio went back to the FBI in Anchorage. Tristan had been a CI for an agent with the DEA, but that guy had turned out to be dirty.

She eyed Crispin. "Maybe one day you can tell me what you do for a living. I'll tell you some stories from when I was a CIA agent."

"Maybe I'll set up an interview, and you can come and work for my company."

Before she could respond, he pushed out of the car.

She used her left hand and kicked the door open. Closed it with her hip.

"You good there, slick?" Rio strode over.

"Good to go." Did he want her to snap a salute?

Rio's brows lifted.

"Fine. I didn't take a pain pill this morning, just some over-the-counter stuff."

"My wife gets grumpy when she's in pain. Or tired. Or when she's hungry. Or when I don't let her help take down bad guys." He frowned. "That sounds like it happens a lot, but it doesn't."

Maria grinned. "Skye is great. Don't worry about it." Sounded like the woman was human rather than the superhero she came across as. Then again, all of the smokejumpers and hotshots were something . . . more than the usual person. It was why she and the boys had fit in so easily.

She looked over at the screen door to the saloon, wondering if today they'd manage to capture Elias Redding. Kane and the boys probably wanted to do it themselves, but as far as she was concerned, she could save them the trouble.

That way, no one would be able to say they'd come after their former teammate in an act of vengeance. Their names would be clear.

The FBI could track down the canister and it would be over.

"Sure you're good? We can have someone else be here in your place."

Maria shook her head. "Elias knows me. If it isn't me, alone at the bar, he won't show."

"All right." Rio ushered her to the front. "Thanks for the intel on the man who hurt you, by the way."

"Hammer passed it on?"

Rio nodded, stopping by the door to say, "He's on the Ten Most Wanted list. A Chinese Triad hitman. A really nasty piece of work. I've got agents tracking him, and they're close to taking him down."

Maria forced her body not to shudder, even though that's what it seemed to want to do. Liquid courage sounded good right now, but what she needed was to keep her wits about her. "Tell me when you have him in custody."

"Will do."

She opened the door herself; he caught it and held it for her as she went in.

"Stay frosty."

Maria headed for the bar alone. Behind the counter, the bartender wore a tank top. She had sleeves of tattoos on her arms and wiped the bar top with a towel. Her hair was dark and shaved close to the side of her head on the left.

"Hey." Maria slid onto the stool, proud of herself for not looking up at the sky when she'd been outside. The name of the game was gonna be focus, like the missions she'd gone on as a CIA operative.

Not as a hotshot with a smokejumper boyfriend.

"Drink?"

"Soda and an order of sweet potato fries."

"Got it." The bartender grabbed a glass and sprayed soda into it.

Maria kept her injured hand in her lap, but no one was going to miss the bandages on her fingers. She was halfway through the fries when a guy slid onto the stool beside her. "I'm expecting Elias. Not you."

"He sent me. That's as good as." A short guy with dark hair.

She slid off the stool, glancing at the militia guy. Pretty sure he was the guy Rio and his people had identified as the person who had stolen the canister the day the senator had been arrested. If he was here, then he probably didn't know where it was now.

But the cops spread all through the room were probably on edge just waiting to grab this guy.

"I don't think so." She started to turn away. As if he wasn't high enough in the bad-guy food chain for her to even consider talking to him.

He grabbed her elbow. "Thought you were here to make a deal."

"I was *here* to meet Elias Redding," she said quietly. "And in a second, I'm gonna be gone and disappointed."

"You think he'd meet you in a place like this?"

She eyed him. "I'm not going anywhere with the guy they hung out to dry. The guy about to get arrested by the cops."

His eyes flared.

"Yeah. Surprise. This place is crawling with cops waiting to arrest Elias. Guess they have to settle for the guy Elias threw to the wolves." She moved her arm from his grasp and set it on the edge of the bar, leaning in a little. "So talk fast. Elias told you to come here? The cops aren't going to settle for anything but you telling them everything you know. They don't give deals out when it's national security. Unless you know where that canister is, where to find Doctor Cortez, and where Elias is right now."

She could sense movement in the room, a shift in the air like growing tension around her, and knew she didn't have much time.

"Where is the canister?"

"Doesn't matter. You'll never find it." His expression shifted, and he looked all smug. "Elias will get that code one way or another."

She said, "I guess he should've come here himself and asked for it."

"They ain't gonna find him. He's too smart to show his face. Guess you should've known that when you asked for a meet."

A niggle of instinct settled itself in her mind. Some of her training, refusing to let her walk away from this guy without working out what was bothering her.

"He sent you. Guess you're a loose end."

Skin around his eyes contracted. He didn't like that. "I'm your warning. You can't stop him."

"Message received." Maria straightened, grabbed her glass from the bar, and finished her drink. She told the bartender, "The FBI will pay my tab. And probably pay for the damage that's about to—"

Rio strode up to them. "FBI. Wilson Cartwright, you're under arrest." He looked at Maria. "What damage?"

The front door of the saloon flung open, and Crew rushed in. "Everyone get down!"

Automatic gunfire exploded outside.

The windows beside the door shattered, blowing glass inside. Rio dragged the militia guy to the floor.

Maria grabbed the counter and clambered over the bar one-handed, landing on the far side, where she grabbed the bartender's arm. "Get low!"

She clapped her hand over one ear and listened to the steady *rat-tat* of bullets eating into the front of the saloon.

Lord, don't let anyone get hurt.

Lord, don't let anyone get hurt. Kane was trying to give it to God, to let go of control. *Do what You need to do to get her attention.*

The plane leveled off, shuddering as it caught an air current.

"Should've let me fly."

Kane glanced over at Saxon. "You've thought about being a pilot for real, right?"

Saxon shook his head. "I don't wanna be told what to do. And I *definitely* don't wanna file a flight plan. It's no one's business where I'm going."

Kane chuckled.

"Got your landing in sight?" Jade stuck her head between their shoulders and looked out. Streamers floated down in the wind.

"Got it, boss."

Jade slapped Kane's shoulders. "Go."

He jumped out of the plane. The line caught, dragging out his chute so that Kane didn't even have to pull the cord. He had his toggles to steer. The terrain stretched out, white-topped mountains. All that endless sky above, full of the haze of wildfire smoke.

One jump, a few other skills, most of which he knew from being a hotshot. No big deal.

Kane didn't want to get cocky, but he could probably do this in his sleep. Sticking on the ground with Maria and being content with that had been the bigger challenge. Now she'd encouraged him to go out and do what he could. She was doing what *she* could—with plenty of highly trained guys to watch her back—and he was going to trust God.

I get it. I need to trust You. I need to let go of a little bit of control and give us both some space.

Kane turned far enough to see Saxon nearly beside him, tracking with him on the way to the landing zone. They'd done this so many times, but not in all this gear. Or with so many other smokejumpers behind them, coming down.

He adjusted course for the air currents and avoided the trees to the west, descending to a clearing about half a mile wide on the side of a hill. About a mile west of the fire. It was moving fast, covering ground, driven by the wind.

It wouldn't be long before the fire was here.

The clearing was barely big enough to land on, but he and Saxon had come up with the plan to get the team down and convinced Jade they could do it.

As he neared the ground, the air shifted, and he smelled something else. Not wildfire smoke.

Not fresh air. Not anything from an animal or any other kind of predator.

"Gasoline." Kane looked around but saw nothing. The fire was a mile to the east, heading this direction. They were supposed to cut a line in this remote area so it didn't spread to the westerly spruce.

His boots hit the ground, and he folded, caught himself, and stood to wrap the chute.

Saxon did the same beside him. "Smells like gas!"

Kane looked around. "I caught it too." He grabbed the radio from his leg pocket. "Boss, it smells like gasoline down here. We might have a problem."

Fire flared up in the trees to the east, erupting like a small explosion, sending smoke up into the sky. Four hundred yards away at least.

Between him and the flare-up, the other firefighters landed one by one in the clearing. Textbook—just like he'd explained to Jade.

Kane stowed his chute in his pack and dragged off his jumpsuit. He sprinted toward the fire, running at the fastest pace he could manage. Across the clearing to a spot where his boots splashed in the wet ground.

He kept running, needing to get a look at the

fire. Not so textbook. He might actually get fired for this.

Scratch that.

He might get *failed* for this.

"Foster!" His radio blared, the voice female and not happy, to say the least. "Get back here!"

Another fireball exploded in front of him, at least eight feet to the right of the previous one. Now a fire. This one ignited a tree and blew it apart, sending pieces all over—including down the side of this steep hill.

He stopped running and looked down at his feet, standing in half an inch of damp ground.

Gasoline.

Another explosion, this one to the south.

Pop.

Pop.

Two more came in quick succession. He turned on the spot, watching fire ignite the trees around them.

Jade tromped up to him. "You'd better have some kind of explanation for this."

"Elias."

She flinched. "That's what Crispin is here to take care of. This is about fighting fire."

"He knew we were coming up here."

She shook her head. "The fire is probably in

the roots, and these old trees are so dry they're snapping. It's crazy, but it happens."

Kane grabbed her shoulders and tugged her around.

A tree exploded in front of her.

"We're surrounded," Kane said. "Elias brought us up here to kill us." He let go of her and strode to Hammer, ignoring the look on his team leader's face. "It's a trap."

"Maybe he'll come to see our grisly end himself." Hammer drew a gun from his pack, his eyes narrow on the terrain around them.

"Everyone gather up!" Jade called them all over.

Kane tromped to her. "Sorry. I know I disobeyed orders, but the ground is soaked with gasoline, and those were rigged explosions. This is no ordinary fire."

She stared at him, coldness in her expression. "Then I guess we'd better do what we do and get it to burn itself out."

"A backfire?" Vince shifted closer to Cadee.

Orion put his arm around Tori. "That could leave us worse off before we starve the fire of vegetation to burn."

Skye and JoJo shifted closer in. Skye said, "We need to call for a retardant drop. Or water."

Hammer and Saxon both looked at Kane. Expressions that probably matched his right now. Determination. The knowledge that this would get worse before it got better.

Kane and Jade. Standing together in the middle of the fire. Facing the fact they could get swallowed up by it.

"We pray and we get to work." Jade lifted her chin. "Skye, get Tucker on the phone. Explain the situation."

As Kane watched, fire flickered to life all around them. It swept across the edges of the clearing, flame coalescing with flame. Growing. Moving. Soaking up the gasoline. Consuming all living things. It would burn away everything and leave nothing in its wake.

Nothing but ash.

Smoke filled the air.

Someone started to pray out loud. Another smokejumper picked up where they left off, and then another, until everyone in the group had asked for favor and guidance. For a way to beat back the flames.

Kane said, "Amen."

Skye stepped away and got on the satellite phone with Tucker, asking for a drop.

Tori started to cough, dragging out tools from

their supply drop that had landed before they'd jumped.

Orion glanced at her but tore open another pallet. "I've got the chain saw."

"We don't want sparks," Jade said. "Hand tools only."

"Got it." He grabbed a Pulaski, and they raced to the trees not yet in flames.

The blaze beat them to it, and they scrambled back.

Vince called out, "We might need blankets!" He grabbed a shovel. He and Cadee ran to a spot on the far side and started shoveling dirt on the fire. Hammer and JoJo did the same nearby, trying to create an exit path. A way through the flames so they weren't pinned down with no way out, choking to death.

"Find a spot already burned that we can hunker down in!" Jade scanned the clearing. "We're surrounded!"

Skye lowered the phone. "Water drop is on the way."

"We need retardant," Kane said. Water wouldn't put this fire out.

"The plane is busy. We can't get it." She strode toward them, a dark look on her face.

"We need to get digging and get everyone out

of this clearing." Saxon looked around, then up in the sky. "Or we're going to get swallowed."

"We don't have time for that." Jade looked around. "We need to deploy shelters. Dig a trench for your face and get down!"

In moments, the fire would race into the clearing, and every inch of ground under their feet would be on fire.

Elias would win.

All because Kane had brought them here. So how had Elias planned all this ahead of their coming to this spot? Unless he'd been orchestrating fires all along, drawing them out so he could eventually kill them.

He grabbed a shovel and raced to the others, hauling dirt away from one spot. He ignored the smell of gasoline in the air and the way the wind seemed to crackle.

Heat rose in the clearing.

Sweat rolled down his face.

Jade said, "Everyone dig a trench! We're about to run out of time." She whipped her fire shelter from her pocket. "You know what to do!"

Tori screamed.

THIRTEEN

MARIA COUGHED. DUST PARTICLES floated in the air. The bartender had paled and looked a little wary of moving, even though the shooting had stopped a minute ago.

"Okay." Maria had to cough again. "We can do this slowly."

"I'm Vic, by the way."

"Maria. Ready?" She held out her good hand.

Vic motioned to Maria's other hand with a lift of her chin. "What did you do to that hand?"

"Had a run-in with a Chinese hitman."

Vic looked like she didn't believe her.

Honestly, Maria didn't blame the woman. "We can go slow, all right?" She turned her head to the side. "Special Agent Parker!"

He called back, "Yeah?"

"You good?"

"It's clear," Rio shouted. "Everyone stay put. We'll assess you one by one." His tone lowered. "I want an update on that vehicle. *Now.*"

Maria winced. Someone had pursued the car outside, surely. Whoever the shooter had been and whatever they'd been driving, they weren't going to get far in a town like this. "Let's get out from behind this bar."

Vic grabbed her hand and they stood, but it seemed like the bartender thought Maria was the one who needed help.

They rounded the open end of the bar, and Maria got a look at the carnage. Whoever had shot at the exterior of the building knew what they were doing. All the windows had shattered, letting in the cool air from outside. Bullet holes in the siding let in beams of sunlight that reflected off all the dust and particles floating in the air.

Tables had flipped over. Stools and chairs. Bottles on the back wall had shattered. Liquid had splashed across the floor along with broken glass and plastic cups.

"Is anyone hit?" Maria looked around.

People started to stir, emerging from where they'd hunkered down.

"Anyone bleeding?"

Rio grabbed up the guy she'd been talking to—the man Elias had sent as a scapegoat, fully intending to kill him along with the rest of them.

Thankfully, Kane and the rest of the smokejumpers were out fighting fire, away from what was happening in Copper Mountain.

Maria went over to . . . what had Rio said his name was? "Wilson Cartwright."

He practically rolled his eyes at her.

"Guess you're nothing but a loose end, just like the rest of us. Expendable."

He made a face.

Rio said, "Tell us where to find Elias Redding and that canister, and I'll talk to the US attorney about forgiving some of the numerous charges you're facing."

Wilson had to think about that for a second.

"Tick, tock." Maria folded her arms, mostly just so she could tuck her injured fingers out of sight. Everything hurt, and she needed more pain meds, but it was much better to look strong even if she didn't feel it.

She'd prayed.

In the heat of the moment, when she'd figured she was about to be killed. Leaving all this business unfinished. Never seeing her father, even though she'd been searching for him for fifteen years. She'd prayed to God because He was the only one who could fix a situation that bad.

Maria wasn't so sure how she felt about that.

She supposed that meant she believed.

Which, to be honest, wasn't so much of a stretch. After all, why would she want to live in a world that didn't have a God in control of everything? All the evil. All the pain. If there was no hope, then why would she want to be here?

She certainly wouldn't want to beg to live.

It hadn't been about self-preservation in that moment. Nor had it been about bringing Elias to justice or saving people's lives—saving the country. It had been about something far deeper.

Hope.

A future.

It had been about Kane.

"I don't know where he is." Wilson looked at the front windows—where they used to be.

"But you know how to find him, right? You have his number. He's the one who ordered you to come here." Rio sounded like the tough FBI agent he was. A guy who wasn't going to back down when lives were on the line.

Maria's eyes filled with tears, but it was just about the dust in the air. It wasn't because she realized that even without her boys here, she wasn't alone. She had the support of people like Rio, Crew, and Tristan. Her friends. Her family.

Even with nothing, she still had everything she needed.

"He has a cabin. It's remote, and no one knows where it is," Wilson said. "So there's no point trying to beat it out of me."

"What if we get a Chinese guy to break a few of your fingers?" Maria said.

Rio glanced at her.

Fine. Maria walked away to the door, where she followed a couple outside. They didn't look banged up, just shaken.

An ambulance pulled up out front, followed by a green-painted rural fire truck.

Crew crouched in front of a young woman sitting on the curb who was holding a napkin or cloth against her forehead.

Tristan was helping a lady out of her car, which had taken a header into a light pole.

She went to Crispin, standing by their vehicle, talking on his phone. She kind of ignored him, got the passenger door open, and sat with her legs out, her feet on the ground. She needed that anchor right now.

Crispin crouched in front of her, still holding the phone to his ear. "Yes, sir." He touched her chin gently, turning her face so he could look at it. "Yes, sir." He held a finger in front of her face and moved it to one side and then the other.

She followed his finger, then closed her eyes.

"Yes, sir. I will do, sir." Pause. "Thank you."

Maria needed to find her own phone, but she had no idea where she'd put it. The day hadn't been a complete failure, especially if no one was seriously hurt.

"I'm sorry, Mr. President, I'm getting another call, and I need to take this." Pause. "Yes, sir."

She opened her eyes. Crispin was on the phone with President White? Never mind, of course he was.

He tapped the screen of his phone. "Hello? Oh, uh . . . yeah. Sure." He held the phone out to her. "It's Raine."

"Put it on speaker."

He tapped the screen.

"What's up, Raine?" After the woman had pretty much tried to murder Tristan, Maria wasn't sure she wanted to hear what Raine had to say. Even if they were teammates. Even if one day she'd understand why and maybe even sympathize. Tristan had stuck around to help Maria. He was across the Midnight Saloon parking lot, walking an elderly man toward the waiting EMTs.

Maria wasn't convinced he'd done anything wrong.

"The smokejumpers are in trouble." Raine let out a breathy exhale, audible through the phone. "My grandfather called me. He said Elias has it all set up. He lured the team out into a clearing so he could kill them."

Crispin's expression hardened. "Jade."

And the rest of them. Maria gritted her teeth. "Where?"

"We can't drive there. That's why they were deployed, because it's too remote to reach on foot or with a vehicle."

"So we get a chopper and rappel in." She would figure out how to do that with her hand.

Raine said, "Mack and Grizz heard the call. They said the train runs nearby, and they think they can get us close. They ran off to the other side of the base here that the BLM runs, yelling about the train."

Maria frowned. "A train?"

"I think they're gonna hijack it and go up the mountain. Try and save everyone."

"Good." Maria swung her feet in the car and grabbed the phone. To Crispin she said, "Get Crew and Tristan. And tell Rio that Skye is in trouble."

Crispin raced away toward the destroyed restaurant.

"Why did your grandfather decide to tell you this now?"

"He feels bad. He doesn't like what the Reddings are doing, but he had no choice. They would've killed him if he'd talked or even tried to get out. But Elias is crazy. My grandpa was a wildland firefighter years ago, when he was young. He doesn't want the team to die."

"Neither do I."

In the background of the call, a train whistle rang out.

Raine said, "Can you meet us?"

"Where?"

"Mile marker thirty-two. There's a turnout on the side of the highway. You'll be able to get on the train there."

"We'll be there."

She hung up in time to see Crew, Tristan, and Crispin race over, Rio right behind them. "The smokejumpers are in trouble. Let's go."

Kane lay still while the fire rolled over him. Crackling. Popping. The heat in the fire shelter made him feel like a potato wrapped in foil and set in a bonfire to cook. Right about now, he was feeling medium rare.

He held still like so many times in his life when he'd been forced to hold the line. To keep steady and wait. If anyone could do it, it was these people he'd been working with all summer. *We can do this.* Their team was solid.

Still, he hummed "Amazing Grace," trying to keep his thoughts focused. He was all the way at the last verse, that slight sound coming from his lips, while in his mind he sang the words at full volume as if he were alone in a small country church.

The only one left.

The earth shall soon dissolve like snow.

Or ash.

The sun forbear to shine.

In winter in Alaska, at least—though this far south they'd have sunlight around lunchtime. It probably felt to the locals as if they lived in darkness.

But God.

Oh boy. That was a whole sermon in itself. *But God.* Wasn't that always, forever, how things began, how they continued each day, steady as the turning of the earth? And how they would come to completion. Those two words set everything to rights.

In his heart.

In the world.

In You, Lord.

He focused his thoughts and kept humming.

But God, who called me here below, will be forever mine.

Forever Yours. Kane had made that choice years ago, the same day his cousin Ridge had made that pledge. They'd given their lives to the lordship of Jesus Christ. Because how else were they going to have peace in their hearts and hope for the best kind of future?

The alternative wasn't worth considering.

Like Peter had said to Jesus: "Lord, to whom shall we go?" He had the words of eternal life, and none other. Where else was Kane supposed to find peace and healing? He hadn't found it.

He'd found Jesus.

No, Jesus had found him.

The distant rumble of an engine broke through his thoughts. Enough Kane braced. He thought he heard someone shout, but didn't hear more. The retardant plane had made it here after all.

Liquid hit the fire shelter, the sensation like a pile of rocks being dropped on him. The chemical that would protect them and dissolve the fire right where it burned. It would keep them safe from being overcome with destruction.

Kind of like what Jesus did with him, giving him a covering, protection from what would destroy everything and leave his life in ruins.

He waited, counting. Forcing himself to stay until he knew for sure it would be safe to get up. Then he moved slowly, inch by inch.

Hot air clouded with ash particles wafted at his face.

Kane coughed, displacing the fire shelter as he sat up. Unhooked it from his feet. Shoved it to one side.

The clearing was black. Thick clouds in the air obscured everything.

He tried to inhale and coughed again.

Someone sat up close by. Dark-blonde hair in a braid.

"Jade!" He scrambled to her, touching her cheek.

She pressed a hand to her front, breathing hard, in and out.

"You good?"

She nodded. "Check the others." Her voice cracked, thick and rough.

Water. They needed water, and a way to call for rescue.

But first, he had to see who was alive and who was . . .

"Call out!" Kane got to his feet and looked around. "If you hear me, call out!"

A fire shelter whipped open to his left. Hammer.

"You good?" He held out his hand and dragged his buddy to his feet.

Vince emerged from the smoke, sweat rolling down his face, what looked like some singed clothing on his left side.

Hammer patted himself down. "Nearly lost the beard." He touched the side of his face where the heat had burned away some of the hair on his chin.

"Come on." Kane waved at the area around them. "Spread out."

Vince, Hammer, and Kane walked slowly out in three directions. Kane watched for the telltale silver glint of . . .

There.

He tugged up the edge and found Orion. The younger guy blinked at him. Kane said, "You good in there, buddy?" He didn't want to call Orion's father and let him know the worst had happened. Charlie had only just found his son last year, and they had so much time still to spend with each other. Charlie needed to see his son get married—to Tori, would be Kane's guess. Then Charlie was going to have grandchildren.

"I'm good." Orion sat up. "Let's never do that again."

"I've got JoJo!" Hammer called out.

"I found Skye!"

"Keep talking!" That was Cadee. "I'm walking toward you."

"Over here, babe." Vince.

"We need to find Tori." Kane's words got Orion up and moving. Kane called out, "Is anyone hurt?"

They called out one by one. No one had any major injuries.

When they were done, Orion said, "Tori!"

No answer.

"Everyone spread out and find her," Kane said. He prayed with each step. Looking on the ground for another fire shelter. Hoping she'd managed to get inside it. "Did you see her before we hunkered down?"

"She was nearby me." Orion's voice shook. "I didn't go that far from her, did I?"

"Keep looking." Kane prayed harder as his

anxiety grew, knowing exactly how Orion felt, because if Maria had been out here, he'd be feeling the same thing.

Finally, he spotted a glint of silver foil in the haze of smoke. "There!"

They raced to her spot. Orion landed on his knees and pulled back the shelter. He sucked in a breath. Tori's shirt had done its job, thickening and carbonizing to create a protective barrier between her skin and the fire. Not perfect, but better than being exposed to flame.

But her face hadn't been so lucky. Skin on her cheek and beside her hair had peeled away, leaving a nasty-looking red patch.

"Tori." Orion brushed her hair back from her shoulder. The guy sucked in a choppy breath. "Tori, wake up."

Kane shifted her to her back, untangling her from the fire shelter, which he dragged away and tossed aside. He crouched on the other side of her and scanned her, then yelled, "Medic!"

Hammer would know what that meant. Kane didn't need to say anything else.

He reached over and felt for a pulse. "She's alive."

Orion didn't breathe.

"We need water." Kane rummaged in his pockets and found a few things, like gauze and a multitool that was hot to the touch. He dropped it on the scorched ground.

Hammer came racing over. He tore open a gauze packet and pressed it to the side of Tori's face. "Is she breathing?"

Kane tilted her chin and turned his head, listening for a puff of air from her nose. *Come on.* He felt a tiny puff of air on his cheek. "She's breathing." He sat up. "We need to get her out of here."

Orion looked like he was about to pass out, seeing the woman he loved like this.

"Hold steady." Kane squeezed the younger man's shoulder. "Keep praying."

Skye and Jade came over. Then JoJo and Cadee. Vince stood beside Cadee. Saxon said something low to Hammer that Kane didn't catch. All of them looked like they'd been through a war.

It was a mercy that only Tori had been badly hurt. Thanks to that chemical drop, they had survived. Everyone was alive and would stay that way long enough to see another day.

To have a chance at a future with the people they loved.

"We need a chopper." Orion turned to Jade. "Call for a pickup. We need to get her to the hospital. *Now.*"

"The chopper can't land in this smoke. It'll choke the engines."

"Then we hike out. Carry her with us." Orion looked like he was about to bust out of his skin.

"We can carry her between us." Kane had rigged a sledge a few times to drag an injured buddy out of the line of fire. They had enough people they could rig something up and each hold a corner. Get her out of here.

Jade nodded. "We'll use a fire shelter."

"Which way are we going to go?" Vince looked around. "How do we get out of here without walking a hundred miles in the wrong direction?"

Orion said, "We only have to get far enough to get picked up."

Kane was all for hiking out, but in their condition and with equipment, it would take too long to pick their way down the mountainside. Not the first time, and God would be with them every step. "We can do it. If we're careful. It'll be slow going, but we aren't going to get out of this by staying put."

Orion nodded.

Kane heard a crackle, down by Tori's hip. Then broken speech. *A radio.* He dug it out and found it hot to the touch. "Ouch." He got the button pressed down. "Hello? Can anyone hear me?"

The handset crackled, and he could hear someone speak, but only broken syllables.

In the distance, a train whistled.

FOURTEEN

WATER HIT THE FIRE, AND MIST evaporated into the air. The entire hillside next to the train blazed with flames. The two water tankers on the train both had spray hoses attached, and Mack had commandeered one. Crew was on the other.

Grizz let loose on the whistle again. Mitch was up there in the engine car with him and the driver and conductor, trying to contact the smokejumpers on the radio.

They weren't dead. Maria refused to believe it.

"You get the feeling this is about boys and their toys?" Raine stood beside her in the open-air car, no windows and just a fiberglass roof above them. "They seemed a little too excited to take the train."

Maria wanted to smile, because both Mack

and Grizz had been overjoyed at the chance to ride a train. They'd convinced the conductor and some other guys to take them on a ride to save a group of smokejumpers when no one else could get to them. Tristan and Crispin weren't far behind them in the open-air car, looking serious and talking quietly. Rio paced up and down the train car, talking on his phone and gesturing wildly.

The special agent still working his case. But he was all in to be here when his wife needed saving. He'd been insistent with his boss that he was going with them—and already in the car when he told his special agent in charge in no uncertain terms why he was leaving the suspect in the hands of the local sheriff.

Raine glanced over at Tristan.

Who just happened to be looking at her exactly at that moment.

"Please tell me you're going to figure things out with him," Maria said. "Before you get arrested for attempted murder."

"I can't believe he covered for me and told Tucker it was him." Raine winced, turning to look out at the trees going by. They weren't able to go as fast as Maria wanted to be going, but it was quicker than she'd be able to manage in this terrain on foot.

The train trudged up the side of the mountain, rounding the edge where this peak met the next and cargo could be transported between Copper Mountain and the more remote communities to the north.

Smoke hung in the air. Probably, if there was no fire, the view would be spectacular. "I'm glad we can't see out that side."

"Steep drop-off." Raine nudged her elbow. "Long way down."

Maria shuddered.

"It's kind of funny that the big bad super CIA agent is scared of heights," Raine said. "You never did that thing in the movies where they run across rooftops trying to escape the bad guys?"

"No." She spotted something in the smoke. Where the mountain backed away from them and across a stretch of ground that wasn't so steep, she saw a group of people. Too far to make out who they were. Huddled together, a glint of silver between them.

"Shame."

"I see them." Maria turned to the others. "I see them!"

Tristan ran to the end of the car and hit a button. "Stop the train!"

They were half a mile away at least, the smoke

in the clearing dissipating enough that she could see more and more every second.

Crew and Mack continued spraying water on the fire around them.

The train brakes squealed. It would take time for the long, heavy vehicle to come to a complete stop. Maria wasn't going to wait that long.

She went to the door at one end of the open-air car and unlatched it. The door swung open and clattered against the outside of the wall. She held on to the frame and stepped down onto the metal step. Still pretty high. Was she really going to jump?

The train continued to slow.

"Uh, Maria . . ." Rio came up behind her.

She jumped.

The ground came up fast. She landed, bending her knees, and didn't go down. *Thank You.* She was going to ignore the slightly throbbing pain in her fingers.

Maria ran up the hill, picking her way over uneven ground and boulders set into the grass. Through the thick smoke, ash still falling all around them, the sun trying to clear the shadows.

It was them.

Kane spotted her running and set off toward her.

She found herself smiling, and as they collided in the middle, he picked her up and swung her around. Maria laughed. She rounded his head with her arms, hanging on for dear life before he set her down.

He was covered in dirt and ash, soaked through with sweat, and a little shell-shocked in his glassy gaze. But he'd never looked better.

The others raced up the hill behind her. Rio caught up Skye. Raine ran to Orion where he, Saxon, Vince, and Hammer had set Tori down. Tristan came over. Crispin and Crew found Jade and JoJo.

"Hammer!" Mack raced up the hill.

The two brothers hugged, slapping each other's backs hard. Hammer squeezed the back of Mack's neck. "Did you steal a train, bro?"

Mack's cheeks reddened. "Grizz helped."

Maria fought back tears. "Is Tori okay?"

"She needs a hospital."

"Let's go." She slid her arms from around Kane's neck, reluctant to let go, but if they had to get Tori seen by a doctor, then there was no time to lose.

A helicopter's rotor blades cut through the sound of the train, which was still in the process of coming to a complete stop.

She tensed. "Is that one of ours?"

A helicopter had shot at them just days ago. She didn't want to have to run for her life to a slow-moving train. That wasn't a great getaway vehicle.

Kane shielded his eyes with his hand. "It's ours." He glanced around. "Everyone back up and make a space!"

Orion crouched by Tori, and Maria saw the other woman open her eyes. She had a bandage of some kind on the side of her face and seemed a little singed, but she was alive.

All of them were alive.

Maria's legs started to sag. Kane caught her. "You okay?"

"Just . . . thankful." Too thankful for words. *Thank You.* Because it was God who had kept them all safe this far. Surely He would continue to do it. She didn't think this thing was fully over. Elias was still out there. The canister. Her father.

Elias had tried to kill them all, but he hadn't won.

She touched Kane's cheek, and while he held her close, she pressed her lips to his. The kiss was full of a whole lot of relief, gratitude, and all those just-happy-to-be-alive emotions that overflowed until tears slid down her cheeks.

"Hey." He swiped his thumbs across her cheeks, wiping them away.

"It's okay. I'm fine."

Kane's lips curled up. "Since you're fine and all . . ."

"What?"

He dipped his head close. "I love you."

Her hand on him tightened reflexively. "That wasn't the plan."

"I know."

"But it's a good ending."

"Yeah?"

The helicopter whipped smoke and debris into the air, swirling her hair around her head. She leaned closer to Kane so she could whisper in his ear. "I love you too."

The guys got Tori loaded in the chopper, and Orion climbed in. Kane held Maria while they waved at the departing helicopter.

"We should get moving or we'll miss the train." Mack grinned.

Hammer laughed, swinging his arm around his brother's shoulders.

"Move it or lose it." JoJo ran ahead of them to the waiting train.

Maria grinned, and they all followed her down the hill, jogging to the open-air car. Crew waited at the top of the steps, holding out his hand and hauling each person on board one by one.

Vince led Cadee to the far end of the car, the two of them talking. Crispin and Jade. Skye and Rio talking close, touching each other's faces. Kissing.

Maria looked away and found Hammer and Saxon staring at her. "What?"

Saxon smirked. "Not a thing."

"You guys are annoying."

They both hugged her.

"Hey, back off." Kane shoved them out of the way.

Mack looked a little lost.

Maria said, "You good, kid?"

He nodded.

She wandered to him, widening her arms. Mack stepped into them, and she gave him a reassuring hug. "All good, yeah?"

He nodded against her shoulder.

"Plus you got to fight a fire from a train."

He backed up from her, grinning. Kane wrapped his arm around her waist.

Raine moved behind Mack, and Maria found Tristan on the other side of the train car, watching her intently. Which was interesting.

"We need to find Elias and finish this." Maria

looked around. "A lot of people could've died today."

Skye pulled away from Rio. "You aren't going to stop me. I'm quitting smokejumping."

Everyone turned to them.

Rio did *not* look happy. "Just like that? We get into crazy situations all the time. You're just gonna give up?"

"I wanna have a family."

Rio's eyes flared.

Skye held out her hand. "What do you say, Special Agent Parker? Do you want to have kids with me?"

Maria figured the answer was probably yes, since they were married, but her asking him was basically adorable. Kane's arm tightened on her waist. *Not going there.* They might have said *I love you*, but that didn't mean the future was set.

Rio took his wife's hand. "I thought you'd never ask."

He kissed her, and someone whooped.

Maria smiled, leaning her head on Kane's shoulder. He kissed her forehead, and he didn't let go.

She hoped he never did.

Kane took the fastest shower of his life and got dressed—including his shoes. Maria had told him why she looked like she'd been rolling around in dust on board that train. He couldn't believe Elias had done that. A two-pronged attack designed to kill them all so he could escape.

He strode out into the living area of the men's cabin, which was full of people. Couples. Brothers. Even Jubal, the dog, was in here with them, sitting on the couch, half in Grizz's lap while Dani gave the long-haired labradoodle pets. Dani was about to go back to Washington DC, her packed bags already in the back of Grizz's car. She was only staying long enough to see what happened next, and Maria didn't blame her for not wanting to leave before this was done.

Over by the kitchen counter, Maria set her mug down. She lifted another and held it out to Kane.

"Thanks." He kissed her, because it was a thing now. Because he could and he wanted to. "How is your hand?" He reined back the surge of attraction that was always there when she was around, and turned to the room, his hips back against the counter. He looked at her, sipping his coffee.

"I took another pill."

The front door opened, so he didn't get the chance to talk about her being in pain and pushing through it. He'd rather she stay and rest than go out with them to find Elias, but it was probably better he didn't say it if she was only going to get mad at him.

Rio came in, holding the door for Raine. "We have intel."

Raine went to a stool in the corner and sat quietly, a sick look on her face. Across the room, Tristan stared at her. The two of them were going to have to figure things out. Kane was pretty sure this had nothing to do with the beef between them and a lot more to do with the issue conflicting with a bucketful of attraction that had caught them both by surprise.

"Raine's grandfather told us where this cabin is. The one Elias is holed up in."

Kane rolled his shoulders, feeling the pull of the scarred skin on his back.

If things went the way he wanted them to with Maria, she would see the damage in all its glory. But maybe he didn't care so much now. He figured everyone was damaged in their own way—whether it was visible or not. She loved him, so he didn't have to worry about feeling weak when she knew exactly what it had felt like being captured.

She'd gone through the same thing and survived.

Maria Sanchez was the strongest person he knew.

"We need an update on Logan and a plan." Hammer glanced at his brother. "You're staying here."

Mack looked irritated and relieved at the same time. Ready to take on the world and fully aware of how much fear came with putting your life on the line for the greater good.

His time would come.

"We need a map." Dani shifted on the couch, as if to stand.

Rio shook his head. "This isn't on any map."

Jamie said, "Logan will be able to receive visitors as soon as y'all are done saving the world. He's awake, but considering the fact he's got to reassess his future as a firefighter, he isn't happy. Now, tell me about the map. We have some intel, right?" She glanced at her brother. "You won't be going in with no idea what you're getting into?"

Saxon looked at Kane.

He shrugged one shoulder in response to his friend's unspoken question.

"You guys are doing that thing again," Maria said quietly. "Talking without words."

"All due respect . . ." he began, glancing from Hammer to look at Rio.

The special agent cut him off before he could continue. "You guys aren't doing this alone. It'll look like you have a vendetta." Rio folded his arms. Badge on his belt. Gun on his hip. "We're doing this officially. With me in the lead."

Kane nodded. "Let's go."

They piled into several cars, those who wanted to be part of it, while a few of the women and Mack stayed back at the base.

Kane sat in the back of the car with Maria while Hammer drove. He looked at her.

"Oh, I know that expression." She reached over and took his hand. "Don't worry, I'll hang back and be safe."

He lifted her hand and kissed it. "Thank you."

She sighed. "I just wish I knew where my father was."

Kane flinched. He let go of her hand and dug out his phone, sending a text to Tucker. "I'm such an idiot. I can't believe I forgot." He hit send. "When I saw your father at the hospital, before you escaped those guys"—he wasn't going to say *before you were tortured*—"I slipped my tracker ring in his pocket."

"I remember you telling me." She stared at him, tears in her eyes. "But now it's been two days."

Kane winced. "Tucker will ping it and get us a

location." His phone buzzed in his hand. "There. He's looking it up now. We'll find your dad."

"I'm glad you remembered."

Kane's phone buzzed. She leaned over to see while the map loaded. Maria said, "That's nowhere near where we're going."

"That's good right? Means he's safe. Hiding."

She bit her lip.

"We'll get him back for you."

Saxon shifted in the front seat and turned to face them. "That is what we promised, right?"

Maria said, "I'm gonna hold you guys to it."

She leaned her head against Kane's shoulder and closed her eyes. Kane met Saxon's gaze and nodded slightly. They were good. She just wanted this thing to be over—as much as the rest of them.

It was more than personal for his team. Elias had torn them apart, tried to destroy them, and in every way he could have, he'd betrayed who they were and what they stood for.

But God, who called me here below, will be forever mine.

Kane had claimed God as much as God claimed him. He'd been chosen, but he'd also made the choice. When both worked together, there was nothing that could pull them apart.

Hammer pulled the car off the highway, and

they wound up a dirt road into the woods. Switchbacks meant Kane spotted the cars in front and the cars behind, a convoy of cops and Feds and them, all going up to take down Elias.

Up the hill, between two trees, the first car exploded.

The hood lifted up from the ground with the force of the fireball, flipping upside down.

"Stop the car!" Saxon grabbed the handle at the top of the door.

Hammer hit the brakes, and they skidded to a stop. He shoved the door open. "Stay here."

Saxon got out as well, and the two of them ran off up the hill.

"Land mines." Maria straightened in her seat. "Like that cabin."

Kane prayed for the occupants of that car. "Like when we rescued you." He swallowed. "And I was captured."

"Same old tricks."

"Elias." He growled the other man's name. "And we trusted him."

She touched his knee. "Now you're going to stop him."

He watched the others swarm around the burning vehicle. How far was it to the cabin? He could make it on foot better than a vehicle, and no one else would have to die.

Kane twisted in his seat.

Before he even spoke, she said, "Go."

He kissed her hard. "I really love you."

"Get him."

Kane got out of the car and decided in that second that Elias had most likely buried mines up the road only—so he'd know when someone approached by vehicle. Gun in one hand, he ran parallel with the winding dirt track, pumping his arms and legs. He raced all the way to the end, where a small structure was barely visible. One of those tiny homes, one bedroom tucked up in a loft. A bathroom under it. Small kitchen area and a living space.

He'd liked them—until now.

"On your six." Hammer came up behind him.

Saxon too, though Kane didn't look.

He stepped to the side of the door. "Rio?"

"All good. But probably ticked, so let's do this before he stops us."

Elias had been *their* teammate. This was their mess to clean up.

Kane squared up on the door and kicked it in.

A man sat on the couch, drinking from a short glass of amber liquid. He didn't even flinch when the three of them entered. Blood coated the front of his abdomen, above his left hip. The guy was pale and sweating. A gut shot. This man didn't have long left to live.

"It's over. You're under arrest." This was the man who'd tortured Maria.

The Chinese hitman sipped his drink, then smiled. "Over?" He winced and motioned to the blood on his shirt. "I already knew that."

"You're done." Hammer strode across the room. "You should've left Alaska when you had the chance."

He chuckled. "I guess you caught me. Too bad it's too late. Someone beat you to it."

Kane frowned. "Where's the canister? Where is Elias Redding?"

"I have no idea." A flicker of something crossed the other man's expression.

Kane said, "Who shot you?"

The Chinese man muttered in Mandarin. "That doctor. He tried to kill me, and he took the canister."

Rio stepped in. "I *was* having a good day." He glanced around and spotted the hitman, realized what condition he was in. "It might get better. It might get worse."

Rio said, "Are you guys done here? Can the FBI finish this?"

Saxon shifted his stance. "He doesn't have the canister. Doctor Cortez shot him and stole it, if he's telling the truth."

"What reason would I have to lie?" The glass fell from his hand and spilled on the floor.

Kane studied this man who had tortured a woman tied to a chair and decided the guy had realized it was over before they'd even come in. After all, he knew he wasn't going to survive this wound.

Someone had shown up—or been waiting for him. Maria's father had taken the canister.

"Talk." Kane faced off with the guy. "Now, before it's too late. For once in your life, do the right thing."

"I'm telling the truth. Cortez took the canister." The Chinese man sneered. "Guess he's gonna deploy it himself. Or sell it to someone who will."

"Where do we find Doctor Cortez?" Rio said.

He sucked in a choppy breath and coughed. Blood wet his lips. "Who cares? It's over for me."

Hammer sat on the coffee table, facing a man who was their enemy. "You aren't dead yet. I need to tell you what I know about Jesus Christ."

Kane left his buddy to preach the gospel to a

man most would think didn't deserve it. But if there was one thing Kane—and all of them—had learned, it was that everyone got the chance at redemption.

He walked outside.

Rio followed him. "It might not be the end I want for that guy, but it's an end."

"Justice comes either way." Kane glanced over.

Rio nodded. "We need to find Maria's father, the weapon, and Elias."

Kane patted his pockets but couldn't find his phone.

"Lose something?"

He looked at Saxon, not answering Rio's question.

"Come on." Saxon ran for the car.

Kane followed after him, pushing the pace, but it was too late. In the line of cars up the winding road . . . there was a space. She had his phone—and the location for her father. And she'd pulled out and driven back down.

Maria was gone.

FIFTEEN

MARIA DROVE SOUTH FOR TWO hours, grateful she had enough gas, even if it seemed weird to thank God for that. Did Christians do that? It seemed trivial, but maybe it was all about the simple everyday things and remembering God was in all of it.

She threaded through Anchorage to the port and a small boat launch on the jetty, where she parked before she even looked at Kane's phone.

He hadn't moved. Her father was still here, on a boat of some kind.

She didn't look at how many missed calls or texts she had.

Enough she'd nearly answered, because so many times when she'd been following directions, another notification had popped up. And another.

Requests for her to stop and wait for them. Pleas. Explanations that the guy who'd tortured her was dead, but not before Hammer had preached the gospel to him and their enemy had repented and accepted Christ.

She was going to need some time, and a lot of explanations from them, before she accepted that. But if one person didn't deserve a second chance, then who could claim they did? She hadn't done anything in her life that meant she could claim she did deserve redemption.

Maria got out of the car, pushing her hair behind her ear when the cool breeze wanted to blow it across her face. She scanned the skyline of Anchorage and the high-rise buildings. So much like a big city compared to where she'd been living. And yet for some, it was barely bigger than a town.

This was it. Her father was here.

She would finally get closure—or at least some kind of answer. Kane didn't need to be here. In fact, she wanted to do this alone. That was why she'd left, not really thinking too much about his reaction or what he'd say about her doing this.

Maria wandered down the pier, scanning the boats.

A white yacht at the end of the row caught

her attention. Not because of the long bow or the level above the rear, where a person could watch the water in front and pilot the boat. Or the Alaska state flag.

It was the name painted on the side.

Valentina.

She stopped to stare at her mother's name. Had to swallow against the lump in her throat. "Mom."

The phone vibrated in her pocket.

Kane could find her. She knew he would. The man had been by her side all this time. And when he got here, she would have what she'd come for.

She grabbed the rail and climbed on board, going to the hatch under the second level and descending the stairs.

"You aren't going to change my mind."

She stepped off the bottom stair and saw him across the room, sitting at a table with a case in front of him. "Hi, Papa."

He flinched.

She hadn't called him that in a long time.

"I'm about to go, so you need to leave. You aren't coming." His face twisted with grief. "I didn't want to see you."

"No? Well, too bad, because I wanted to see my father." The phone vibrated in her pocket again. She shifted it in her pocket so it didn't dig into her, but she was going to ignore it for now. "I've been looking for you for fifteen years."

"I know."

That was it? "You know? I watched them drag you away. I stood there while Mom bled out on the ground, and I had nothing left. They sent me to live with Aunt Leticia in Boston, where I'd never been before. I lost everything."

"And I spent fifteen years as a captive, traded for what I know."

"Now you're out. Congratulations, you're free." But he was sitting here. "What are you waiting for?"

"The end."

Maria frowned. "Explain it to me, because I'm trying to understand this, and I'm coming up blank." She shifted, and her hand bumped the wall. Pain whipped through her fingers, and she sucked in a breath.

"I'm sorry you got caught up in it."

"I'm not. I was looking for *you*."

"I told you not to find me."

"That note?" And a conversation with Kane she'd barely known about. "You should have come to me." She slapped a hand on her front. "But you didn't, because you're a coward."

He rose out of the chair. "I'm a lot of things, but a coward isn't one of them."

"No? Prove it." She sucked in a sharp breath. "Tell me what you're doing. Why you have a boat with Mom's name on it, and why everyone is convinced you're working *with* Redding and not doing everything you can to stop him."

"You think I didn't want to escape every single day? That I didn't want to find you?"

"You managed one of those."

"It took everything from me."

She stared at him.

"I have to finish this, and it doesn't have anything to do with you."

"What are you talking about?" If he explained it, then she could help him. But he didn't seem to want anything to do with her. Just like that day when her mother had been shot in front of her and her father dragged away, the foundation of her world shifted.

God, I need You.

And Kane. But God would always be enough, whether she had anything else or not.

"I'm going to destroy the canister. I'm going to take it where no one will find me, and end this once and for all."

"Just destroy it now. Get rid of it. Or turn it over to the cops."

"And then what?" His eyes flared with frustration. "I wait for the next person to snatch me from my life and kill someone I love? I get traded around again? They won't let me live. I'll always be a target for what I know and what I can create. No." He shook his head. "This ends."

"I'm not going to let you die. I already lost Mom."

"You won't dissuade me."

Maria shifted her weight from one foot to the other, ready to argue. She could knock him out. Take the canister. Do this herself. Hide him somewhere no one would find him. Let him live his life. Protect him like the Trouble Boys had done for her. "I know people. I can protect you."

She wasn't going to ask them to spend their lives watching out for him. But she could figure some kind of situation where he went into hiding. Like witness protection.

"If you let me, I can help you. You can get your life back."

He stared at her, hope blooming into a tiny flicker of life in his expression.

Then his eyes flared.

Someone came down the stairs behind her.

Maria turned, but she wasn't quick enough. Elias Redding slammed into her and knocked her into the table.

She fell to the floor, crying out. Kane's phone tumbled from her pocket, onto the floor between her hands, a call in progress.

She turned in time to see her father jump at him. The two of them wrestled with each other, stumbling into the little kitchenette. She gasped. "Dad!" Maria scrambled to her feet and grabbed the case from the table. "This is what you want, isn't it?"

Elias stilled. He kicked her father in the knee and turned to her.

"It's what you've always wanted." She held it up, incapacitating herself, because she had no free uninjured hand to defend herself if he came at her. "You can find another doctor."

"Not like him." Elias took a step toward her. "I think I'll have both of you this time. That way he'll keep in line. Otherwise, I'll hurt you."

Her stomach clenched. "No deal. Take the case and go."

"Or what?" He took another step.

She wasn't sure and hoped he didn't push it. Maria didn't move. Her father didn't move.

A crack splintered something that sounded

like thick plastic, and Elias jerked. Blood ran from a hole in the center of his forehead, and he slumped to the floor. Dead.

Maria stumbled back and landed in a chair.

Footsteps thundered down the stairs. Kane first. He scanned the room, then zeroed in on her and came over. Rio stepped over Elias and went to her father.

"He was trying to be free." Maria didn't care that tears spilled from her eyes and rolled down her cheeks.

Rio looked at her. "We heard your conversation. I'll take care of your father."

Maria nodded.

Hammer and Saxon were there. They stood on either side of Kane. Hammer crouched in front of her. "Can I have that case?"

She didn't want it.

Maria shoved the case at him. Hammer and Saxon left, and she lifted her gaze to Kane, who didn't look happy. "Are you mad at me?"

He pressed his lips together. "Ask me tomorrow." He held out a hand. "Come on, I don't want to stay down here with him."

Maria let him help her to her feet. Before he turned away, she wrapped her arms around his middle and held on. "Thank you."

He wound his arms around her. "Don't leave like that again."

"I won't. I promise."

"I'm gonna hold you to that. Forever."

She lifted her chin and looked at him. "Good."

"Doctor Cortez?" Kane stood at the entrance to the conference room in the Anchorage FBI office. Not a big place, but they were able to be effective here in Alaska. Rio was probably going to get some kind of commendation or a promotion after taking down Elias Redding and recovering a dangerous biotoxin before it could be used in an attack.

No mention in the media of a group of Delta Force soldiers who were supposed to have died two years ago in Syria.

Kane wasn't looking forward to that paperwork or the fact they'd have to surrender themselves to the Army for a debrief at best—a court-martial far more likely. Either way, it would be a long conversation but the chance to tell their story to the authorities.

No one would've believed them two years ago that the Reddings had been working with the Chinese on a way to destabilize the US. Now that they had stopped it and all the players were dead or in jail, it didn't seem so strange.

Maria's father looked up at him. Who knew how long the man had been sitting here alone in a leather chair in this conference room? Waiting to find out what deal the US government could offer him.

They'd considered him a threat. Now they were going to help him?

Kane wasn't sure he would be comfortable with that if it were him. But that was why he was here. "Hi, Rodrigo. It's good to see you free."

The older man's brows rose. "Am I?"

"Depends."

"On?"

Kane eased the door shut. "If you trust the Feds to keep you safe. Or if you want to take a chance on the guy who's been protecting your daughter for two years."

"I know what you are to her. I saw it."

Kane didn't want to be nervous, but this was her father. He was pretty sure he was supposed to ask for permission under normal circumstances. "And you disapprove?"

Rodrigo shook his head. "Quite the opposite."

Kane relaxed a fraction, thankful he didn't

have to be so nervous now. "She's in the hospital getting checked out."

"Good. She hit that table pretty hard," he said.

Kane hadn't seen it, but he'd heard the whole conversation after the call he'd made suddenly connected. It had taken him a minute to realize they didn't know he could hear and she wasn't talking to him. Then he'd used it to give the others with him intel on entering the boat and taking down Elias.

Things could have ended far differently.

Kane said, "My friends and I have been watching out for her for two years. That has to count for something when I say that I have a way you can disappear. I have a friend. He's connected. I mean to the top." Crispin was . . . Kane didn't even fully understand what the guy's job was. Not officially. "This won't be witness protection. It's a job, if you want it. A life, and the understanding that the US government will be protecting you. Off the books."

"In exchange for me continuing to create deadly substances."

"I was instructed to be clear that the job is optional, but it is in the country's best interest to ensure your safety. You can work for the sake of the stability and peace of the world, or you can not work another day in your life. That choice will be up to you."

Crispin had discussed it with Kane, Hammer, and Saxon when they'd turned over the canister to him. Kane had pointed out that it was safer to know where the guy was and what he was doing.

"You will likely be monitored. But that goes both ways. You get to feel safe, and so does President White."

Rodrigo's eyes flared. "I've always liked that guy."

Kane smiled.

"And if I accept this offer? The FBI will let me go and I disappear?"

Kane tipped his head to the side. "We have to sneak out the fire exit. There's a car in the alley waiting for us."

Rodrigo chuckled. "This is the life my daughter has chosen?"

Kane felt his cheeks heat. "I guess so." He coughed, not really sure what that was supposed to mean.

"Very well. I'll choose it also." Rodrigo stood. "I choose life, Mr. Foster." He held out his hand.

Kane shook it. "Welcome to the family."

The older man chuckled.

Kane sent a text. A minute later, Crew and

Tristan came in the front door of the Anchorage FBI office, arguing loud enough Rio stepped out of his office and went to go see what the fuss was about. It also drew the attention of two admin staff members and another agent.

Kane and Rodrigo hurried down the hall and used the exit door, climbing into the back of the rental Toyota. Hammer hit the gas, and they peeled out of the alley. "Hospital?"

"Drop me off." Kane looked at Rodrigo. "Would you like to say goodbye? It might be a while before you two see each other again."

"Perhaps you could tell her I've missed her greatly, and we could set a date. For dinner or some such."

Saxon coughed, and it sounded interestingly like the words *wedding invitation.* Which wasn't what Kane needed to be thinking about right now.

"I can do that." Kane nodded.

Hammer pulled up in front of the hospital, and Kane went in alone. He got directions to Maria's room and detoured to the gift shop. One giant teddy bear and a bouquet of flowers and he was ready.

He knocked on the door.

"Come in." Her voice was muffled.

He eased the door open, and she stirred on the bed. "Did I wake you?"

She shook her head, rubbing her eyes with her good hand.

"How are your fingers?"

"You're just going to ask that and ignore the fact you're holding half the gift shop?"

Kane frowned. "It's not that bad." He walked to the bedside. "Some company." He set the bear by her side and then handed over the flowers. "And something to make the room brighter."

She eyed him. "Are you okay?"

"Me? Sure." He settled on the edge of the bed, smoothing down the blanket by her side.

"You're nervous. You're making it weird! I knew this would happen."

He knew how to fix that.

Kane leaned down so their faces were close. "Want me to drag you onto my lap and kiss you again?"

Her eyes flared. "Flowers are fine."

"Your dad accepted the offer. He wants to have dinner, or anything really. He wants to see you."

"Thanks."

He kissed her gently. "You're welcome."

"I have a couple of cracked ribs."

"Ouch."

"They're going to make me stay overnight for observation."

"Want me to bust you out? Crew and Tristan taught me how to do it."

She chuckled. "I was thinking more like pizza and a movie at the hospital. Until they kick you out."

"They can try and kick me out. They'll find out it's not that easy."

Maria touched his cheek, her fingers warm. She scanned his face. "Was he okay?"

"He seemed . . . better. Maybe he's just resigned to still having limited choices because of who he is. But the point is, he gets to decide for himself now. He won't be a prisoner. More like . . . a guest of the US government."

"Where is he going to live?"

"I guess we'll have to find out," he said. "Do you want to be nearby?"

"What do you want?" She paused. "We get our lives back. Where do you want to go now that you're alive again?"

"Last Chance County. At least for a visit."

"Good, because I want to meet Ridge."

Kane said, "I'm trying to persuade him to come up for the end-of-season party once they get the

Midnight Sun Saloon fixed up. I heard you guys did a number on it."

Maria winced. "It was pretty well destroyed."

"We'll help fix it up."

"Thanks."

"Hey, we said we were in it with each other. You help me, I help you. I figure it's worked pretty well so far."

"Plus you love me," she pointed out.

"Hmm. I think I did say that. Well, you know, it was in the heat of the moment, so there's no telling—"

Maria tugged the pillow from behind her head fast enough to whip it around and whack him upside the head before he finished talking.

"Fine! I yield!"

She quit pummeling him with the pillow.

"I love you."

"Just checking."

Kane grinned. He helped her put the pillow back behind her head and kissed her again. "I'll say it every day if you want to hear it."

She eyed him.

"Every hour. Every minute."

"That might get tired. You wouldn't want to wear it out."

"I love you."

She chuckled. "Good, because otherwise this would be an awkward conversation, and I'd get my heart broken again. I'll be crying in my Bible study tomorrow morning, reading all those weepy psalms where King David is crying and telling God he's gonna slap all his enemies in the face."

"Or . . ." He dragged the word out. "You could read all the verses about kindness and joy."

"Hmm. I guess I could do that." She dragged over the bear and hugged it against her. "For the sake of the bear."

Kane laughed.

"I love you."

He leaned down so their noses were touching. "Good."

"Saxon and Hammer are never going to let us live this down."

"I don't care."

She smiled. "Good. I don't either."

EPILOGUE

Six weeks later

MARIA FLEXED HER FINGERS, FINALLY free of the splint that had immobilized the broken bones until they healed. She walked out of the doctor's office, into the waiting area.

Kane stood, setting aside the magazine he'd been reading. "How did it go?"

She lifted her hands. "All good."

Kane said, "I'll grab the car and pick you up out front."

"Thanks." She settled up with the receptionist and then headed outside, checking her phone as she went.

Her father had sent her another voice message, so she tapped the button to play it and listened to him say, "Well, you were right about that oatmeal. It is much better made with milk than with water." He sounded like he was smiling. "I just wanted to tell you that."

She tapped the button to reply with her own message. "I just got the all-clear from the doctor about my fingers. The breaks are all healed, and I only need to keep up with physical therapy."

She didn't need the steady hands of a surgeon or a professional safe cracker, but it would be good to have her fine-motor control back.

She added, "I think we're going to the end-of-season party now, so I'll catch you up on that later. Love you, Dad."

Maria pushed out of the lobby doors where Kane was already at the curb. She took a second and just marveled that she had her father back in her life and they were working on getting to know each other again. And not only that, but she had Kane.

God had given her everything she'd dreamed of—and so much more.

She slid into the passenger seat.

"Good?"

She nodded. "Let's go."

He drove through Copper Mountain to the Midnight Sun Saloon, newly refurbished with all the damage repaired. The hotshots and smokejumpers who'd been able had spent the end of the season working with the Bureau of Land Management teams. They'd been all over, with Kane at the center of it working as a smokejumper.

Maria had been working on some things that could be next steps for her career, since she had to find a new job now. She had been offered a couple of positions—one at Jamie's company and another working remotely for the organization that employed Crispin.

One was corporate security. The other got her closer to wherever her father was living, in a way.

Kane held her hand, and they walked into the fixed-up bar and grill.

The crowd turned at their entry and a cheer went up.

JoJo came over, laughing. "Don't get too excited. They're doing that for everyone."

Crew came up behind her and slid his arm around her. "Did you decide?"

Maria said, "Did you?"

Kane shifted. "What's this?"

Maria smiled at him. "Crew wants to work at the jump base over the winter before he tries out for the hotshots next year."

"And Maria needs to decide if Crispin's offer is good enough for her."

Maria shoved Crew's shoulder, laughing.

Music started up from the jukebox in the corner. She watched Orion tug Tori onto the dance floor, her face still healing. But Tori had told her that she wanted to get back to smokejumping next year.

Vince walked Cadee onto the dance floor as well.

"Those two have come a long way from arguing every minute of every day," JoJo said. "Like some other people we all know, who turned out to be humans, not just superheroes."

Maria waved a hand. "Yeah, yeah."

Crew dragged JoJo over to dance.

Across the room, Skye and Rio sat at a table, their heads close. Maria said, "You think they're talking about baby names already?"

Kane chuckled, probably thinking it was too soon, but Maria knew a secret only the girls on the team knew.

Saxon, Mack, and Hammer played pool across the room. Mitch and Tucker, their wives, and the jump base pilot and spotter chatted at a table.

Maria spied a T-shirt that said *Last Chance County* and gasped. "Is Ridge here?"

Kane said, "First, I think you need to tell me about Crispin's job offer."

Maria turned and slid her arms around his waist. "It isn't an operator position. It's admin and logistics. Some travel, some schmoozing with Department of Defense bigwigs. Stuff like that. He made it sound super boring, and I can work remotely. Wherever . . . we are."

"Hmm. *We.* I like the sound of that."

She kissed him. "I thought you might."

He'd spent two weeks in Georgia with the Army before coming back to finish out the season smokejumping. They hadn't talked about what he wanted to do next.

"Where might *we* be?"

"I'm still figuring that out."

"Did Hammer talk to you?"

Kane nodded. "He and Mack are going back to Colorado, and Saxon is gonna go with them."

"Their hometown?"

"Renegade Mountain."

Maria said, "We should go visit them."

"I already said we would." He took her hand and led her to two guys wearing matching black shirts with LCC Fire Department on them, close to where Logan sat on a stool. Logan's health had stabilized, but he wasn't ever going to fight fire anymore. He'd accepted a position as incident commander with Cal Fire and started in a couple of weeks.

Maria had seen a photo of Bryce, Logan's twin brother, before. He was dating Penny, Tori's sister, who stood close by, talking to Jamie. Both of them started laughing.

Logan lifted his chin, and the two firefighter guys turned. Bryce stayed by his brother while the other man approached them, a look of awe on his face. Ridge Foster had Kane's build and green eyes but a side part in his darker blond hair.

"My cousin, the hero. Back from the dead." Ridge grinned, an edge of sadness in his eyes.

Kane burst out laughing. "You think I'm gonna die for real and leave you to have all the fun without me?" He let go of Maria's hand and hugged his cousin. It started out with a lot of manly backslapping that sounded painful, but they settled in quickly. Hanging on to each other. Brothers, even if they were cousins. Two men who'd grieved losing each other.

Kane cleared his throat. "Good to have you back."

"You too, bro," Ridge said.

Maria swiped under her eye. "You guys are adorable." They'd missed each other, even if they'd been able to text and communicate in other ways some.

"And your girl, here with you." He shoved Kane aside playfully and held out his hand. "Ridge Foster. Charmed to meet you."

She set her hand in his, laughing. "Nice to meet you as well."

Kane slid his arm around her, severing the hand hold. "Get your own girl. You can't have mine."

Ridge gaped, astonished, but it was clearly only pretend. "How dare you insinuate I would try and convince her to run away with me?" He glanced at her. "Do you want to? You know, just in case."

Maria just laughed.

Bryce slung an arm around Ridge's shoulder, grinning. "He's working on things with his own girl, but she's . . . prickly."

Kane said, "No progress?"

Ridge frowned. "Both of you owe me a drink. I said don't mention Amelia."

Maria chuckled, but not much, because Ridge seemed like he might be genuinely hurt by this woman and her reluctance to see how he felt about her. Whoever this Amelia woman was, Maria hoped she was ready for what happened next.

She looked at Kane, then at his cousin. "I can

tell you honestly that it's worth the wait. No matter how long it takes."

Kane hugged her from behind, his chin on her shoulder.

"So don't give up."

Ridge mouthed *thank you.*

Across the room, Tucker stood. "Can I have everyone's attention, please?"

They all turned, and the music shut off.

"It's been a long hot summer, and we've been through the fire. Some of us literally."

A quiet chuckle moved through the crowd.

Tucker continued. "But in every moment, God was with us all. His amazing grace sustains us and brings us home."

Someone yelled, "Amen!"

Maria said quietly, "Amen."

Kane kissed her cheek.

Tucker lifted his glass. "Let's party!"

THANK YOU

Thank you so much for reading *Burning Justice*. We hope you enjoyed the story. If you did, would you be willing to do us a favor and leave a review? It doesn't have to be long- just a few words to help other readers know what they're getting. (But no spoilers! We don't want to wreck the fun!) Thank you again for reading!

We'd love to hear from you—not only about this story, but about any characters or stories you'd like to read in the future.

Contact us at www.sunrisepublishing.com/contact.

BONUS NOVELLA

To celebrate the conclusion of our Chasing Fire: Alaska series, we want to gift you with a Bonus Novella by Lisa Phillips, a short story about Tristan and Raine, available only to our newsletter subscribers.

This Bonus Novella will not be released on any retailer platform, so get your free gift by scanning the QR code, and enjoy!

Hotshot firefighter Raine Josephs has spent years building a new life with the Midnight Sun crew—far from her toxic family legacy. But when she discovers that Tristan Winters, the mysterious man living at their base, killed her father during a militia takedown, her carefully constructed world explodes.

Tristan never expected to fall for the one woman who has every reason to hate him. A former confidential informant seeking redemption, he's finally found his shot at an honorable life in Copper Mountain. But first, he needs Raine's forgiveness—something that seems impossible when she confronts him with a gun and fury in her eyes.

As Raine grapples with losing her beloved grandfather to cancer and facing a future truly alone, her dangerous ex threatens to drag her into his criminal escape plans. When Antoine tries to kidnap her to use as leverage, Tristan must prove that some risks are worth taking—and some people are worth fighting for.

With domestic terrorists closing in and time running out, Raine must choose between revenge and forgiveness. Can two broken souls find redemption in each other's arms, or will the sins of the past destroy their chance at love?

A finale novella for the Chasing Fire Alaska series set against the rugged beauty of Alaska, where love burns hotter than wildfire and second chances come to those brave enough to reach for them.

Want more Chasing Fire?
Check out this romantic suspense thriller, Flashpoint by Susan May Warren.

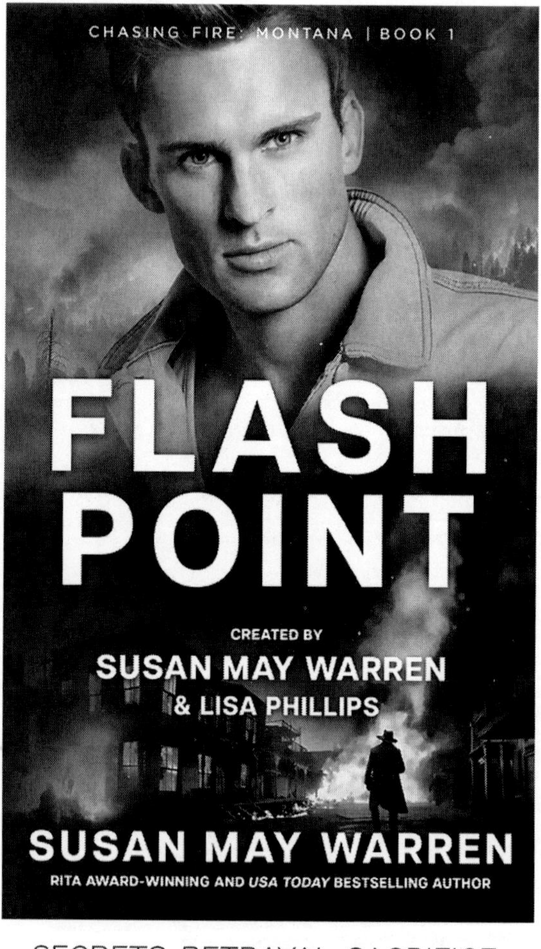
CHASING FIRE: MONTANA | BOOK 1
FLASH POINT
CREATED BY
SUSAN MAY WARREN
& LISA PHILLIPS
SUSAN MAY WARREN
RITA AWARD-WINNING AND USA TODAY BESTSELLING AUTHOR

SECRETS. BETRAYAL. SACRIFICE.
THIS TIME, THEY'RE NOT JUST FIGHTING FIRE.

The Hollywood heartthrob and the firefighter with a secret...

Rookie firefighter Emily Micah is determined to prove herself as a new recruit to the elite Jude County Hotshots wildfire team. Assigned to the film set of The Drifters, Emily's mission is to protect the cast and crew from the special effects that could ignite the tinder-dry Montana forest and start a wildfire.

If only her favorite actor—TV star Spenser Storm—wasn't getting in her way.

What could go wrong?

Haunted by the memory of a rabid stalker, former child TV star Spenser Storm is hoping to revive his career, but he's torn between the glitz and glamour of Hollywood and the life of a cowboy on his family's ranch in Montana. It doesn't help when he sees the movie that's supposed to launch his future is going up in flames.

And then there's beautiful and brave Emily Micah, who not only saves his life, but seems to understand him, maybe better than she should.

As an arsonist threatens the film production, seemingly with the goal of destroying the movie entirely, Spenser realizes he'll stop at nothing to protect his future and the woman now stealing his heart.

But Emily harbors a secret...one that could destroy the flame between them. And when it comes out, it could cost them everything, and ignite an inferno that could destroy all of the northern Montana forest.

ONE

CLEARLY, HIS LAST HOPE AT A COMEback was about to crash and burn.

Maybe he was being a little melodramatic, but Spenser Storm knew a good story.

Knew how to cater to an audience, knew when a script was a disaster.

And this one had flames all over it.

Yes, the screenplay had all the right ingredients—a winning western retelling of a widow and her son who leaned on the help of two strangers to save her land. And they were shooting on location in Montana at a real abandoned western town rebuilt and redressed for the movie, complete with a jail and a church.

They'd even hired an up-and-coming country music star to write original music.

The problem was, the producer, Lincoln Cash, picked the wrong man to die.

Not that Spenser Storm had a say in it—he'd been given all of sixteen lines in the one-hundred-twenty-page script. But he wanted to ask, while waving flags and holding a megaphone—*Who killed off the hero at the end of a movie?* Had no one paid any attention to the audience during the screening of *Sommersby*?

He didn't care how many academy-acclaimed actors were attached to this movie. Because everyone—even he—would hate the fact that their favorite action hero ended up fading into eternity. And he wasn't talking about himself, but the invincible Winchester Marshall.

Perfect. Spenser should probably quit now and go back to herding cattle.

"Back to ones!" Indigo, the first Assistant Director, with her long black hair tied back, earphones around her neck, raised her hand.

Spenser nudged his mare, Goldie, back to the position right outside town. Sweat trickled down his spine, and he leaned low so a makeup assistant could wipe his brow.

Yeah, something in his gut said trouble. It didn't help that all of Montana had become a broiler, even this early in the summer—the grass yellow, the temperature index soaring, turning even the wind from the pine-saturated mountains into the breath of hades.

But saving the movie wasn't Spenser's job. No, his job was to sit pretty atop his horse and smile for the camera, those gray-blue eyes smoldery, his body tanned and a little dusty, his golden-brown hair perfectly curled out of his black Stetson, his body buff and muscled under his blue cotton shirt and a leather vest.

He wore jeans, black boots, and could have walked off the set of *Yellowstone*. No, *swaggered* off the set. Because he wasn't a fool.

They'd cast him as eye candy. With sixteen lines and the guy who got the girl at the end. Spenser was the sizzle for the audience who was too young for Winchester Marshall, the lead of the movie, although Spenser was just a couple years younger.

But, like Lincoln Cash said when he signed him, Spenser had a special kind of appeal.

The kind that packed the convention floor at comic cons around the world.

Wow, he hated comic cons. And adults who dressed up as Iwonians and spoke a language only created in fanfic world. If he never heard the name Quillen Cleveland again, he'd die a happy man.

He hated to mention to Lincoln that the fans who loved *Trek of the Osprey* might not enjoy a western called *The Drifters*, but a guy with no screen credits to his name for five years should probably keep his mouth shut when accepting a role.

At least according to his agent, Greg Alexander.

Keep his mouth shut, deliver his lines, and maybe, hopefully, he'd be back in the game.

"We need a little more business from the extras." Director Cosmos Ferguson wore a *Drifters* T-shirt, jeans and boots, and his own cowboy hat. "Feel free to cause more havoc on the set."

Behind him, Swen, from SFX stepped out of the house, checking on the fire cannons for the next shot. The set crew had trailered in an old cabin for today's shoot—a real structure with a porch and a stone chimney that rose from the tattered wooden roof—and plunked it down in a valley just two hundred yards from the town, with a corral for the locally sourced horses. It was a postcard of bygone days.

Was it only Spenser, or did anyone else think it might be a bad idea to light a fire inside a rickety wooden house that looked already primed for tinder?

"Quiet on the set!"

Around him, the world stopped. The gaffers, the grips, the second team, the stuntmen, even, it seemed, the ripple of wind through the dusty one-horse ghost town-slash-movie set.

Not even Goldie moved.

"Picture's up!" Indigo said.

At least Spenser could enjoy the view. The sky stretched forever on both sides of the horizon, the glorious Kootenai mountains rising jagged and bold to the north, purple and green wildflowers cascading down the foothills into the grasslands of the valley.

"Roll sound!"

A hint of summer night hung in the air. Perhaps he'd grab a burger at the Hotline Bar and Grill in Ember, just down the street from Motel Bates, where the cast was staying. Okay, the lodging wasn't that bad, but—

"Action."

The extras, aka cowboys, burst to life, shooting prop guns into the air just before Winchester Marshall, aka Deacon Cooper, rode in, chasing them away with his own six-shooter. They raced out of town, then Deacon got off his horse, dropped the reins, and checked the pulse of the fallen extra. "Hawk, C'mere. I think this is one of the cowboys from the Irish spread."

Spenser's cue to ride on screen, dismount and confirm, then stand up and stare into the horizon, as if searching for bad guys.

Seemed like a great way for a guy to get shot. But again, he wasn't in charge of the script.

So, he galloped onto the set, swung his leg over Goldie's head, jumped out of the saddle, and sauntered up. He gave the scene a once over, met Winchester-slash-Deacon's eyes with a grim look, and nodded. Then he turned and looked at the horizon, his hands on his hips, while the camera zoomed in, trouble in his expression.

"Cut!" Cosmos said as he walked over to them. "I love the interaction between you two." He turned away, motioning to Swen.

What interaction? Spenser wanted to ask, but Winchester—"Win" to the crew—rose and clamped a hand on Spenser's shoulder. "One would think you grew up on a horse the way you rode up."

"I did," Spenser said, but Win had already turned away, headed to craft services, probably for a cold soda.

"Moving on. Scene seventeen," Indigo said. "Let's get ready for the house fire."

Spenser jogged over to Goldie and grabbed her reins, but a male stunt assistant came up and took hold of the mare's halter. "I've got her, sir."

Spenser let the animal go and headed over to the craft table set up under a tented area, back from the set, near the two long connected trailers brought in for the actors. The Kalispell Sound and Light truck was parked next to an array of rental cars, along with the massive Production trailer, where the wardrobe department kept their set supplies, including a locked container for the weapons.

"That was a great scene." This from the caterer, a woman named Juliet, whose family owned the Hot Cakes Bakery in Ember. She wore her brown hair back in a singular braid and handed him a sandwich, nodding to drinks in a cooler. Not a fancy setup, but this far out in the sticks, they were beggars. Cosmos had also ordered a hot breakfast from the Ember Hotline every morning.

"Thanks." Spenser unwrapped the plastic on his sandwich. "This bread looks homemade."

"It is. The smoked chicken is from the Hotline, though." She winked, but it wasn't flirty, and continued to set out snacks—cookies and donuts.

The sandwich reminded him a little of the kind of food that Kermit, the cook for the Flying S Ranch, served during roundup, eaten with a cold soda, and a crispy pickle.

Sheesh, what was he doing here, back on a movie set? He should be home, on his family's ranch . . .

Or not. Frankly, he didn't know where he belonged.

He turned, eating the sandwich, and watched as lead actress Kathryn Canary, seated on a high director's chair, dressed in a long grimy prairie dress, her blonde hair mussed, ignored a makeup assistant applying blood to her face and hands. She held her script in one hand, rehearsing her lines as Blossom Winthrop, the heroine with Trace Wilder, playing the role of her husband, Shane Winthrop.

Who was about to die.

He hadn't seen Trace since his last movie, but the man seemed not to remember their short stint on *Say You Love Me*.

Spenser would like to forget it too, frankly. Another reason why he'd run back to the family ranch in central Montana.

It all felt surreal, a marriage of Spenser's worlds—the set, busy with gaffers setting up lighting, and the sound department fixing boom mics near the house, the set dresser putting together the scene. And then, nearby, saddles lined up along the rail of a corral where horses on loan from a nearby ranch nickered, restless with the heat.

Cowboys, aka extras, sat in holding with their hats pushed back, drinking coffee, wearing chaps and boots. All they were missing were the cattle grazing in the distance. Maybe the smell of burgers sizzling on Kermit's flat grill.

Bandit, the ranch dog, begging for scraps.

They did, however, have a cat, and out of the corner of his eye, Spenser spotted Bucky Turnquist, age eight, who played Dusty Winthrop, chase the tabby around the set. His mother, Gemma, had already hinted that, as a single mom, she might be interested in getting to know Spenser better.

Now, she talked with one of the villain cowboys, laughing as he got on his horse.

"You guys about ready?" Cosmos had come back from where the cameramen were setting up, the grip team working to shade the light for the shot, on his way to Kathryn and Trace, who were rising from their chairs.

One of the SFX guys raised a hand from where they set up the cannons that would 'fire' the house. Not a real fire, not with the burn index so high in this part of crispy, dry Montana. But enough that it would generate heat and look real.

And enough that they'd asked the local wildland fire team on set to keep an eye on anything that might get out of hand. He'd caught sight of the handful of firefighters dressed in their canvas pants, steel-toed boots, yellow Nomex shirts, and Pulaskis hanging out near the fire. They'd brought up a fire truck, too, with a hose ready to deploy water.

"Get a hose over here, Emily!" A man wearing a vest, the word Command on the back, directed a woman, her blonde hair in a tight ponytail, to pull up a hose nearer the building, and hand it over to another firefighter. Then she ran back to the truck, ready to deploy.

According to the script, the cowboys would fire at the house, and then a stuntman would run out, on fire, and collapse to the ground. Cue Kathryn, as Blossom, to run in with a shirt she'd pulled from the hanging laundry to snuff it out while the cowboys attempted to kidnap her.

She'd panic then, and scream for Dusty, and only then would the kid run from the barn.

They'd be surrounded, swept up by the villains and taken away while poor Shane died.

At which point the guy would go down to the Hotline for a nice cool craft beer and a burger, then tomorrow, catch a ride to Kalispell and head back to his air-conditioned apartment in LA.

"Ready on Special Effects?" Indigo shouted. She'd reminded him that this wasn't *Trek of The Osprey* and that he wasn't the star here when he'd headed to the wrong trailer on day one.

Whatever. Easy mistake.

"Ready!" This from Swen, who stood away from the house. The cowboys were already in place and Blossom stood at the clothesline in the yard, away from the house.

"Quiet on set!" Indigo shouted. She glanced at Cosmos, who nodded. "Roll Camera. Roll Sound."

A beat. "Action!"

And that's when he spotted little Bucky, still chasing the cat, scooting under the house on his hands and knees.

At the front of the house, a window burst and flames licked out of it.

"Wait!"

The next window burst. More fire.

"Bucky's in there!" Where was his mother? It didn't matter. He took off for the back of the house.

The cowboys in the front yard whooped, shots fired, and of course, the stuntman stumbled out in his firesuit and flopped onto the front yard.

Blossom screamed and ran to put out the fire just as Spenser reached the back of the house.

The fire seemed real enough, with the roof now catching. "Bucky?"

With everyone's gaze on the action, no one had seen him wriggle under the porch. Spenser hit his knees. "Bucky?"

There. Under the middle of the house, curled into a ball, his hands over his ears. "Bucky, C'mere!"

He was crying now, and Spenser saw why—the entire front porch had caught fire.

Sparks dropped around him. The grass sizzled.

Aw—Spenser dropped to his belly and army crawled into the center of the house, coughing, his eyes watering. He grabbed Bucky's foot, yanked.

Bucky kicked at him, split his lip. Blood spurted.

"C'mon kid!"

He grabbed Bucky's arms and jerked him close, wrapping him up, holding him. "It's okay. C'mon, let's get out of here." Smoke billowed in from where the porch fell, a line of fire blocking their escape. But out the back—

Then, suddenly, a terrible crack rent the building, and with a thunderous crash, the old chimney tumbled down. Dust and rock crashed through the cabin, tore out the flooring, and obliterated the porch.

Blocked their exit.

Spenser grabbed Bucky and pulled him close, holding his breath, then expelling the dust, his body wracking with coughs. And Bucky in his arms, screaming.

When he opened his eyes, fire burned around them, a cauldron of very real, very lethal flames.

"Stop! Stop the film! There's someone inside there!"

Or at least Emily thought so. She still wasn't quite sure if that was a person or an animal she'd seen dive under the burning house.

In truth, she'd been stationed by her fire truck, watching the house burn, trying not to let her gaze drift back to the beautiful and amazing Spenser Storm, standing near craft services.

The Spenser Storm.

From *Trek of the Osprey*. Quillen Cleveland in the flesh, all grown up and ruggedly handsome, dressed in western getup: leather vest, chaps, black boots, and a Stetson over his burnished golden-brown hair, those gray-blue eyes that a girl could get lost in. He even wore that rakish, heart-thumping smile. The man who saved the galaxy, one world at a time, there he was . . .

Eating a sandwich.

She'd spotted him almost right off this morning when she'd arrived with fellow hotshot Houston James and her fire boss, Conner Young. The Special Effects department had called in the local Jude County Hotshots as a precaution.

Not a terrible idea given the current fire index.

The SFX supervisor, Swen, had briefed the hotshots before the event—squibs of dust on a lead that would explode to imitate bullets hitting the building. They'd walked through the system that would create the explosion, a tank filled with propane, rigged to burst the window and release a fireball.

She'd expected the bomb, but when the squibs detonated, Emily nearly hit the dirt.

Nearly. But *didn't.* So, take that, panic attack. No more PTSD for her, thank you ten years of therapy.

Except, the explosion hadn't gone quite like they'd hoped. Sure, the gas dissipated into the air, but somehow cinder had fallen onto the porch.

The entire old wooden porch burst into flames.

Black smoke cluttered the sky, and if she were a spotter, via a fire tower or a plane, she'd be calling in sparks to the local Ember fire department. Which would then deploy either the Jude County Hotshots or, if the fire started further in, the Jude County Smokejumpers. The first and last line of defense against fire in this northwest corner of Montana.

About as far away as she could get from her failures, thank you.

Not anymore. This was a new season, a new start, and this time . . . *this time* the shrapnel of the past wasn't going to eviscerate her future.

So, she'd stood by the truck, waiting for the signal from Conner. Tall, brown hair, calm, he'd been brought in to command the team for the summer while Jed Ransom, their former boss, now crewed the Missoula team.

And that's when, in her periphery, she'd spotted—was that a *person* diving under the back of the house? Black boots disappeared under the footing of the cabin.

Were they out of their *mind?*

Maybe it was an animal—cats sometimes ran toward a fire instead of away.

"Boss!"—She had nearly shouted, but that would carry, and with the house on fire, the director only had one take. Instead, she'd headed to the house—

The chimney simply collapsed. A crack, then

thunder as the entire handmade stone chimney crumbled. She dropped to her knees, her hands over her head, as dust, rock, and debris exploded out from the house.

From the front came shouts and shooting, the cameras still rolling. She lifted her head, blinking as the dust settled. The inferno now engulfed the front of the house, moving fast toward the back, the roof half-collapsed. "Boss!"

And then a thought clicked in—*black boots.* "It's Spenser! Spenser Storm is under the building!"

No one heard her over the roar of the fire, the shouts from the street.

No one died today. Not on her watch.

C'mon, Emily, think!

She ran over to the truck, grabbed her Pulaski, and then opened the cab door and hit the siren. It screamed over the set as she scrambled toward the house.

Flames kicked out the side windows now, the heat burning her face. She pulled up her handkerchief and dug at the rubble.

The siren kept whining, sweat burning down

her back, but in a second, she'd created a hole. She dropped to her knees. "Hello? Hello?"

"In here!"

Smoke cluttered the area, but she made out—yes, Spenser Storm, and a kid.

Oh no, the little Turnquist kid, the son of one of the locals in town.

Emily's eyes watered, but she crawled inside the space, pushing the Pulaski out in front of her. "Grab hold!"

Hands gripped her ankles. "Emily! Get out of there!"

Conner's voice.

"Grab the ax!" she shouted.

Spenser's hand gripped the ax, his other around the kid.

"Pull me out!" this, to Conner.

It was everything she could do to hold onto the Pulaski as they dragged them out from the crawl space. She cleared the building, then launched to her feet even as Conner tried to push her away.

Spenser Storm appeared, like a hero crawling from the depths of hell. The child clung to him, his face blackened, his wardrobe filthy and sooty, his eyes reddened, coughing as he kicked himself free.

"Bucky!" His mother ran toward him, but someone grabbed her back.

Instead, superstar Winchester Marshall, aka Jack Powers, aka whatever hunk he was playing in this western, was right there, pulling the kid from Spenser's arms.

Cosmos pushed through to grab Spenser, helped him to his feet. Spenser bent over, coughing.

"Water! Make a hole!" Cosmos yelled, leading Spenser away.

The movie star didn't even look at Emily as he stumbled to safety.

"C'mon—we need to put out this fire." Conner took off for the hose.

She ran to the truck, still coughing, turned off the siren, then, seeing Houston's signal, she hit the water.

The hose filled, and in a moment, water doused the house, spray saturating the air.

She leaned over, caught her knees, breathing hard. Watched as the fire died. Listened to the roaring on set, and in her heart, subside.

Felt the knot unravel.

No, no one died today. Especially not Spenser Storm.

She stood up, still hauling in breaths. She'd *saved* Spenser Storm. Holy cannoli.

No, no she wouldn't make a fool of herself and ask for an autograph. And certainly not tell him, ever, that she'd had at least two *Tiger Beat* centerfold posters of him in his Osprey uniform—a pair of black pants, boots and white shirt, leather vest, holding a Vortex Hand Cannon. Never mind mentioning that she'd once attended a Comic-Con just to stand in line for a photo op. He wouldn't remember her, right? Or her status as a Stormie—a member of his official fan club?

"Hey!"

She looked up. Froze.

Spenser Storm was headed her direction, holding a water bottle, his eyes watering, looking like he'd just, well, been pulled from a fire. "You okay?"

She nodded, her eyes widening. C'mon words—

"I just wanted to say thanks." He held out

his hand. "You saved my life back there. And Bucky's."

She nodded again. *C'mon words!*

"Maybe I can buy you a drink down at the Hotline sometime?"

"Mm-hmm." *That didn't count!*

Then he smiled, a thousand watts of pure charisma, sunshine and star power, winked, and walked away.

And right then, right there, she nearly died.

Lisa Phillips is a USA Today and top ten Publishers Weekly bestselling author of over 80 books that span Harlequin's Love Inspired Suspense line, independently published series romantic suspense, and thriller novels. She's discovered a penchant for high-stakes stories of mayhem and disaster where you can find made-for-each-other love that always ends in happily ever after.

Lisa is a British ex-pat who grew up an hour outside of London and attended Calvary Chapel Bible College, where she met her husband. He's from California, but nobody's perfect. It wasn't until her Bible College graduation that she figured out she was a writer (someone told her). As a worship leader for Calvary Chapel churches in her local area, Lisa has discovered a love for mentoring new ministry members and youth worship musicians.

Find out more at www.authorlisaphillips.com.

WE THINK YOU'LL ALSO LOVE...

Fire Department liaison Allen Frees may have put his life back together, but getting the truck crew and engine squad to succeed might be his toughest job yet. When a child is nearly kidnapped, Allen steps in to help Pepper Miller keep her niece safe. The one thing he couldn't fix was the love he lost, but he isn't going to let Pepper walk away this time.

Expired Return by Lisa Phillips

Stunt double Vienna Foxcroft's stunt team are the only ones she trusts. Then in walks Sergeant Crew Gatlin and his tough-as-nails military dog, Havoc. When an attack on a film set sends them fleeing into the streets of Turkey, Vienna must face the demons of her past or be devoured by them. And Crew and Havoc will be tested like never before.

Havoc by Ronie Kendig

When an attempt is made on Grey Parker's life and dead bodies begin piling up, suddenly bodyguard Christina Sherman is tasked with keeping both a soldier and his dog safe... and with them, the secrets that could stop a terrorist attack.

Driving Force by Lynette Eason and Kate Angelo

Made in United States
Cleveland, OH
06 August 2025

19148309R20180